Under the Table

ALSO BY STEPHANIE EVANOVICH

Big Girl Panties

The Sweet Spot

The Total Package

Under the Table

A Novel

Stephanie Evanovich

HARPER LUXE

An Imprint of HarperCollinsPublishers

HarperCollins books may be purchased for educational, business, or sales promotional use. For information, please e-mail the Special Markets Department at SPsales@harpercollins.com.

FIRST HARPERLUXE EDITION

ISBN: 978-0-06-288758-0

HarperLuxe™ is a trademark of HarperCollins Publishers.

Library of Congress Cataloging-in-Publication Data is available upon request.

19 20 21 22 23   ID/LSC   10 9 8 7 6 5 4 3 2 1

For John—thanks for the laughs. And the love.

Chapter 1

Zoey Sullivan didn't mind the cold. She liked the feel of the wind in her hair, even when it bit at her ears and made her nose run. It encouraged her to walk briskly, just like natives of the Big Apple did. Since Zoey had arrived from a Cleveland suburb nine months ago, she made it her mission to avoid the "tourist stroll." Not only did it aggravate people hurrying to get where they were going, but she also had been sufficiently convinced the night before she left Lakewood, Ohio, that slow walking made you a target of thieves, rapists, muggers, and murderers that lurked on every corner. So, when her phone started vibrating in her coat pocket, she ignored it. *Don't pull out your phone, don't flash any cash. Walk confidently with your head up and purpose in your eyes. Ax the headphones. Keep a loose but firm grip on your bag, like there is nothing important in it.*

Keep moving, even when walking down Park Avenue on the Upper East Side. Anyone not sporting a border-line sneer is either being watched over by someone else or carrying a weapon.

While growing up, she was often accused of taking things too literally.

Zoey's phone vibrated again and she picked up her pace, this time sticking her free hand into her pocket and around the phone while her other hand tightened around her magic bag. Surprisingly, she was unable to identify the caller through telepathy. Then it shook again. It became a series of one vibration after another, a veritable calling frenzy. What if it was her appointment canceling on her? The very thought was a mixture of disappointment and relief. Zoey ducked into a Duane Reade and pulled out her cell phone. There were only two callers, her sister and an unknown number. Neither had left a message. As she looked down at her phone, her older sister's name became visible on the screen and the phone shook again. Her sister did love her drama, as long as it wasn't too real.

"Ruth," Zoey answered, "I just left our apartment a half hour ago. Why are you calling me every thirty seconds?"

"Not me." A snicker came through the phone followed by the warning. "I've been waiting a minute or two. I wanted to make sure you weren't caught off guard."

Ruth and Zoey were the oldest, born a year and a half apart, in a family that inadvertently ended up with six children. Not originally their parents' plan, but they were passionate people who often threw caution to the wind when Barry White came on the radio. All their siblings were welcomed and loved, even if money sometimes got tight. Their mother had read every book on parenting available in those early years, before her hands became permanently full, and had acted accordingly. The firstborn is the perfectionist, the serious one, the rule follower. The second (and last child if it had gone according to plan) was supposed to be the quirky daredevil, who faced life fearlessly, the risk taker.

The only problem was, nobody told the girls. Zoey got the whimsical name; Ruth got everything else. Well, not everything. Zoey got the pretty face and attention to detail; Ruth got the rocking bod and the swagger. Ruth was carefree and vivacious, perfectly content grinding out her nine-to-five inputting insurance claims for a big company in the financial district and cutting loose every weekend. She broke hearts like peanut shells and could break a bone on any would-be assailant just as fast. Ruth lived setting her own rules and without regrets. The boss at her first job when she was eighteen learned that lesson the hard way, along with the one about keeping your hands to yourself. After settling out of court what would have been a hefty sexual harassment lawsuit, Ruth packed up and never thought about Ohio again. She was so much damn fun, when she offered to let reserved, cautious Zoey become her roommate, it was a no-brainer, even if Zoey did have to acknowledge she was living vicariously through her sister . . . and some- times woke up to nearly naked stockbrokers, lawyers, and/or piano bar players roaming around their Lower East Side apartment.

"What's up?" Zoey got to the point after Ruth's ominous leadoff.

"Derek figured out you got a cell phone."

Zoey closed her eyes tight for a few seconds, leaning against the cap at the end of the candy aisle until she felt it start to give way. She quickly straightened back up, her grip tightening around both the phone and her precious bag.

No, no, no . . . this is not what I need today. At least now Zoey had a pretty good idea who the unknown caller was.

"Zoe?" Ruth asked when she got no immediate answer.

"Yeah, I'm here. What did you tell him?"

"Right now, I'm sorry I answered the phone, but he's becoming a pest. I don't mind lying by omission. But he flat out asked me if you had gotten one. I told you once you started screening his calls on the landline that he was going to know something was up."

Zoey knew Ruth harbored a soft spot for Derek, probably because they both embraced their selfish sides. "What did you tell him? Did you give him my number?"

"Of course not!" Ruth sounded slightly put off. "I don't ever give out anyone's cell phone number without their permission. But I did promise him I would ask you if it's okay."

"Well, you know the answer to that."

Zoey heard Ruth's heavy sigh. "I'm too late. He did recite me your correct number, but I swear I didn't give anything away. I just said that I would ask you."

"I have one caller other than you. It keeps coming up as unknown. I don't think there is a scam in the world that wants to robocall me that much." Irritation whistled through her teeth. "This is the last thing I needed today."

"You're going to have to talk to him eventually. He is your husband."

"Only because he doesn't know when to quit." Zoey was loud and quick with the response. After noting the glances in her direction from other, usually aloof Duane Reade shoppers, Zoey brought her tone back down to a whisper and took a few steps toward the door. "I can't deal with this right now. And I'm creeped out enough as it is."

"Ah. The secret customer with his penchant for all things NOLA," Ruth said, back to being jovial. "Maybe he's the one who's been calling?"

"Nope. I have him in my contacts by name."

"Of course you do."

"What is that supposed to mean?" Zoey snapped with pent-up tension. She wasn't the one who collected phone numbers for a hobby.

"I just meant that you're as conscientious as ever. Get ahold of yourself, little sis. Don't worry, I remember what you told me to do. If I don't hear from you by three that everything is on the up-and-up, I'm to call you. And if I get no answer, then call the police to tell them that you've been abducted by the Craigslist Crawdad Killer."

Ruth was making too light of a situation she thought was serious. Zoey gave a quick "That's right. Gotta go or I'm going to be late. Thanks for the heads-up." Zoey pushed the END button on the phone, cutting off Ruth's follow-up. Then she powered the phone down, even though that meant there would be no way to track her if she was kidnapped and thrown into the trunk of a car in the next twenty minutes. She dropped the phone back into her coat pocket and pushed the drugstore door open. She was back on the street. There was no problem with the pacing, since she felt the all-too-familiar urge to run. She also no longer appreciated the chill; all she felt was the heart-pounding flush that came with the feeling of having no control.

Zoey didn't want to admit it, but just the mention of a potential return of Derek Sullivan into her life was enough to turn her inside out. And she was already on shaky ground since accepting a job offer from one Tristan Malloy.

It started innocently enough, with a phone call inquiring about private catering. Zoey had placed the ad on Craigslist and other NYC-based platforms in the hopes of appealing to small dinner parties and wealthy romantics who wanted something a bit more intimate than making reservations. She had no official culinary training, just an honest love of cooking and a large family to experiment on. Once she broke free from the Midwest and Derek, she drove her twenty-year-old Chevrolet Cavalier through the Lincoln Tunnel into the electric, pulsating city. When the car promptly seized up and died on Forty-Second Street, the song playing on her radio was "Empire State of Mind" by

Jay-Z and Alicia Keys. And if her dreams of conquering the concrete jungle included watching her car get towed away for scrap as soon as she got there, then she was off to a great start. She took it as a challenge. Zoey knew within weeks of working in a cubicle three floors down from Ruth that an office job was never going to cut it. But she was a terrible singer and all of the acting jobs in town were probably taken, so she settled on trying to make something out of the hobby that she loved. Within the first month of running the ad, she had yielded a kid's birthday party where she tested her skills on chicken nuggets and hot dogs with fries for ten kids who were only interested in the cake, a pseudo BBQ for some foreign exchange students from Turkey, and a jerk-ball who upon their first meeting asked her if she was going to be the dessert at his dinner. So much for conquering the concrete jungle. Still, Zoey refused to be daunted. Thanks to her sister's vast network and her own word of mouth at the monotonous day job, she soon was booking all her weekends. Four months later, she was able to abandon the nine-to-five, pay her half of the rent, and still have something left over. She even scored a few regular customers. She had three months to prove she could make it on her own. None of it prepared Zoey for when the landline rang last week.

"Good evening. May I please speak to the person who placed the advertisement for a personal chef?"

"Speaking," Zoey sang, then, not recognizing the voice, she dialed it back to a more professionally courteous, "My name is Zoey. And I just need to clarify, I'm more like a private caterer."

"May I ask what you see the difference as?" the caller asked politely.

"Well, a personal chef is usually a full-time position with a single client. I'm more along the lines of the person you call when you want to impress your boss or a date. A full-fledged caterer would be able to feed as many people as you want, but I max out at about twenty guests." Zoey wasn't doing a very good job at selling herself, but the leering perv who wanted her to jump out of a cake was impossible to erase from her mind. And she thought it vital that whoever was on the other end of the line know she was her own boss and wanted to remain that way. "May I ask who I'm speaking to?"

"Certainly, please excuse my bad manners," the masculine voice continued. "My name is Tristan Malloy. And I'm not looking for a personal chef, at least not yet. Can you prepare Cajun food?"

Not yet? One of her pet peeves was people who assumed if they offered her something, she would automatically want it. This man sounded different. Zoey had never gotten much further than looking up a Cajun recipe, but she did know how to read and measure, and she always had her little bag of tricks. "Mr. Malloy, that happens to be my specialty. Would you like to set up a meeting to discuss a menu and I can quote you a price?"

"A meeting won't be necessary. I'm interested in a five-course meal, including sorbet, with a Cajun theme, not too heavy on the fish. For myself and seven guests. Nothing that requires a lobster bib or can get a person messy. Just the staples are fine, you don't have to go overboard with creativity. Are you available next Thursday?"

She was; her work mostly filled up her weekends. That served a dual purpose. She made money and had a built-in excuse for preventing her sister from dragging her all around town. She wanted to take this time in NYC to clear her head, not cloud it further, and it was working for her. But this whole conversation was becoming highly unorthodox. He didn't want to meet her, wasn't asking for references. He wanted to give her free rein. "I do happen to have that day open. I would need a few hours to work up a price quote."

"Would it be possible to give you my number and you can call me back with the details?" the ultrapolite Tristan Malloy asked, making Zoey all the more intrigued, and slightly suspicious. She wanted to insist on a meeting, to verify that he wasn't wasting her time with some prank.

"Do any of the guests have food allergies?" Zoey asked.

"Not that I'm aware of. Let's keep away from peanuts, just in case. Shellfish should be fine for at least one course. Mix it up though?"

"Would you like me to email you the details so you can have them in front of you as we chat?" Zoey offered.

There was a long pause before "That won't be necessary. Just call me back with your final total. Feel free to add the cost of a server on too."

Zoey made a mental note to bump up the price and do the serving herself. She could present to eight people with her eyes closed. And a man who wasn't interested in dickering about the price probably had a nice kitchen . . . or was a psychopath. She took his phone number then checked the expiration date on the can of pepper spray she'd bought when she arrived but had yet to use. Why didn't he want an email? Everyone wanted some sort of confirmation in writing. That was just good business. Unless it's someone who doesn't want to leave a trail. A chill ran through her and she chastised herself for watching too much *Law & Order: SVU*.

Zoey did her research and called him back with a menu of Shrimp and Sweet Potato Bisque and Broccoli Salad for starters; Sausage Jambalaya, Crawfish Mac & Cheese, and green beans for the main course; with a bread pudding for dessert. She recommended lemon sorbet for the palate cleanser.

He listened patiently and then there was a pause after she wrapped up her spiel, quoting him two prices, one with him providing the food and one if she had to buy it.

"Don't worry about having to purchase the food, Zoey," Tristan said. "But the mac and cheese dish is a bit much if you're serving it with jambalaya. Let's switch that up with an eggplant and corn casserole I have a recipe for. If you would be so kind as to fax me the rest of the menu and the ingredients that you need at this number, I'll make sure it's all here when you arrive."

Zoey knew what she'd be doing this week. Trial running recipes. But she had to admit, the eggplant and corn dish sounded delicious.

It also wasn't unusual for a customer to buy their own ingredients to prevent her from marking them up. But fax him? It was so odd. Tristan Malloy didn't sound like a dinosaur. After taking a minute to wrack her brain about where she might find a fax machine,

Zoey remembered Ruth's office had one that was gathering dust. "Is it all right if I get it to you tomorrow, Mr. Malloy?"

"That will be fine."

He gave her his address and a noon arrival time. Before hanging up, he added, "And, Zoey?"

"Yes, sir?"

"Please call me Tristan. I look forward to meeting you next week."

And then he was gone and she was left staring at her landline's receiver.

Zoey spent the days leading up to Thursday buying a cell phone and trying to anticipate all the things that could go wrong while Ruth teased her for being overly paranoid. Then when she tested the recipes she had chosen, the end result on some of the dishes was less than she had hoped for. By the time she was ready to leave the apartment, she was strung tight as a drum. Now Derek was incessantly calling a cell phone number he wasn't supposed to know. It added a layer of foreboding.

She should've insisted on a meeting. Then she wouldn't be walking into this whole situation blind. But he sounded so . . . what was the right word? *Polite*? *Honest*? *Shy*? Maybe the word she was looking for was *innocent*. If Zoey wanted to take advantage of him, she would have no problem doing so. It was the levelheaded politeness that had set her off-kilter. Now was not the time to let her guard down.

Zoey made her turn onto East Seventy-Ninth Street and began looking at building numbers. When she found 139, she breathed a small sigh of relief. A beautiful high-rise, complete with front awning and a doorman. If she was walking into some sort of trap, at least there would be a witness who "saw her last."

She announced herself and the older man with the row of shiny buttons didn't call up to any apartment, just directed her to the end of the hall on the twelfth floor.

Zoey got off the elevator, taking her first few steps. She hated the huge buildings with the long hallways. They were broken up by nothing but closed doors, waiting to pop open as she passed them. It was eerily quiet, and with each of her footfalls on the carpet getting her closer to her final destination, she could almost hear "Redrum" in the background.

This is just another job. Get ahold of yourself.

She reached the end of her walk, took a few center-ing breaths, and lightly rapped on the door.

Chapter 2

There was no immediate answer. After waiting thirty seconds, Zoey lifted her hand to knock louder, but before she could, the door opened.

She tilted her head at the spectacle standing before her. Her eyes tried to take it all in at once, but it was too much. Between the bright, silky, salmon-colored polo shirt and the plaid pants that were interwoven with the same color as well as teal and purple stripes, she fleetingly wondered if a Cajun clown had been hired to answer the door. It was March—maybe there was a whole Mardi Gras theme going on.

"Zoey?" the man in neon plaid asked. "Hi. I'm Tristan. Come on in."

"Hi, Tristan," she replied, remembering his request to drop the formalities while stifling a laugh. All the worrying seemed silly now. "It's a pleasure to meet you. I hope I'm not too early."

"You're right on time. Dinner isn't supposed to be until seven, but I wanted to give you time to acclimate yourself to the setup. Can I take your coat?"

He opened the door wider. She stepped into the foyer, looking down at the floor, until she was sure she wouldn't break out into a fit of giggles. Half expecting to see him wearing red, floppy shoes, she was relieved to see standard white sneakers. By the time she looked back up, he was already leading the way through the living room toward the kitchen. She followed behind him, watching his long strides. Thanks to the pattern of the pants, she couldn't tell where his butt ended and his legs began. He was dressed bright enough to be located in an avalanche.

Tristan pushed a swinging door and her breath caught in her throat. What a magnificent kitchen it was, and she had been in enough kitchens to know.

Recently remodeled, it was a paradise of granite, gleaming chrome, and stainless steel. There were dozens of spotless white wood cabinets. Cabinets that were so high, even six-foot-plus Tristan would need a step stool to reach the top shelves. It smelled of coffee and freshly baked cookies.

"I was going to pull out pots and pans, but I figured you would want to explore the space yourself," he commented while opening two drawers in the center island. "There are both warming and refrigeration drawers here. I turned them on for you."

He had to know he possessed a kitchen worthy of the culinary gods, despite the nonchalant way he moved across the room and pointed out the twin Sub-Zero refrigerators stationed side by side with paneling that matched the cabinets.

"I put everything from your list in this one," he said while opening the one on the left. It was fully stocked and shelved neatly. He closed it and then regarded her curiously. Zoey had yet to utter a word, still bowled over by the room itself. She couldn't wait to start opening drawers and turning on burners.

"Do you carry that around in case you inadvertently poison someone?" he asked, gesturing to the bag she still held in her grip.

This time Zoey didn't hold back the giggle. The old worn-out doctor's bag was the first purchase she had made when she decided to go into business. She had found it in a secondhand store in the East Village. She placed it on the nearest counter, where it looked woefully out of place in such a shiny space.

"I call it my magic bag, but it really holds my apron, knives, a clean shirt, and spices," Zoey explained. "Spices are the key to unlocking flavor. Unfortunately, if anyone gets food poisoning, they're going to need more help than I can give them. I do taste all the food before I present it, so I'll be going down for the count with the rest of you."

"Now that's what I call dedication," he quipped, adding a small grin.

Zoey liked him already. "I'm not doing such a great job at building your confidence with my abilities, am I?"

"I wouldn't call it your strong suit."

"I can only promise I haven't poisoned a client yet." She held up a hand in pledge.

"Then you're doing just fine. I like honesty. And a doctor is on the guest list tonight."

"If you point him out to me, I'll serve him last. Just in case," she teased back, and he laughed.

It was then that Zoey got her first good look at Tristan, without the distraction of the clothing. She placed him at close to thirty. His hair was a little nerdy, too long, with a part straight down the middle. Somehow it suited him. It was full and brown, highlighted by either the sun or John Frieda. His eyes were green, already showing crinkling on the outside corners. His clean-shaven chin was strong. There was simply no way to judge his physique given his current state of dress, but he was lean enough to tuck his shirt into his pants. There was a cuteness to him, but she'd be hard-pressed to classify him as sexy. His voice was deep and strong, but not overbearing. His laugh was welcoming. Zoey couldn't think of anyone less intimidating than her newest client.

He was giving her a quick once-over too, she could tell. She hoped he could see beyond her hazel eyes, figure that showcased her love of food, and brunette hair that no matter how many times she had it cut always found its way back to the curls she had in her teens. She wanted him to see beyond the exterior to all the things she was—intelligent, confident, and con-scientious. He wasn't leering at her, it was more like a brief yet thorough assessment.

"I'll let you get settled in," he suddenly said, turning on his heel and pushing through the swinging door. "Holler if you need me."

Left alone in the gorgeous kitchen, Zoey's first in-stinct was to spread her arms open wide and give a twirl, like Julie Andrews did when the hills came alive. But she'd end up looking like a loon, so she opted for pulling out drawers and opening cabinets to familiarize herself before starting to get down to work.

He had every utensil a gourmet chef could want, all neatly lined up in rows in the drawers next to the six-burner stove. Both Calphalon nonstick and top-of-the-line stainless-steel pots and pans were housed in spacious drawers beneath it. There were multiples of every size of mixing bowl and matching serving dishes she could imagine. She opened up a cabinet next to the stove and found all his spices. Dozens of labeled glass jars, again neatly marked and rowed. She took a quick inventory.

"There is no way this guy has his own fenugreek," she said under her breath, right before her gaze settled on it, right in between the jars of fennel seed and garlic powder.

Alphabetized spice cabinet and exceedingly easy to work for. This guy was a treasure. Zoey thought she might actually wet herself and left the kitchen in search of the bathroom, unable to recall if she had passed one on the way in.

She stepped into the living room and stopped. Tristan was standing in front of a big picture window, feet slightly apart. He wasn't admiring the view, he was looking down at his feet, his hands loosely balled, one resting on top of the other. He shifted his feet from side to side then swiftly pulled his arms across his body and to the right, hands still together and eyes still downcast, before swinging them to full extension on the opposite side, his eyes finally lifting. There were two things that became clear to Zoey. The first was he played golf, which explained the clothing. The second was that with the stretching of his body, the silky shirt was tightly flush against his torso. The result was the detailing of some sleek abdominal muscles. His biceps and triceps clearly defined.

The verdict was in—golf clothes made for outrageous fashion statements and were designed for comfort and not style, unless the wearer was aiming for bizarre. Zoey cleared her throat to get his attention. His hands dropped back to his sides as he turned to her. Not startled per se, but like he had been forced out of deep concentration.

"Sorry to interrupt. I was just looking for the powder room?"

"Right down the hall. First door on the left from where you came in." He went back to lining up his golf swing.

When Zoey returned to the kitchen, Tristan was waiting. Now he was wearing a purple visor and a matching windbreaker.

"I have a one-thirty tee time in New Jersey. I want to leave you a key to the apartment in case you need to run out for anything," he said, placing the key next to her now-unneeded spice bag.

"That's not necessary. You seem to have more than enough of everything." Zoey picked up the key and tried to hand it back to him.

"Take it anyway," he politely insisted. "Just in case you need a breath of fresh air."

He had an awful lot of trust for someone who lived in the city. Never once had she ever been left alone in a client's home. Maybe someone else was here? She didn't want anyone sneaking up and surprising her.

"If I have to leave, maybe your cleaning lady can just let me back in? Or your wife?"

His curious look was back, only this time he added a pair of pursed lips. "I don't have either one of those."

"I'm sorry," Zoey said quickly. "I'm not used to someone leaving me alone in their home, especially after knowing each other ten minutes."

"Were you planning to rob me?"

"Of course not!"

"In that case, I should be back by five, five thirty at the latest. Make yourself at home," Tristan said over his shoulder as he left. Zoey waited to hear the front door close before shoving the key in the front pocket of her standard black serving pants. When dealing with food, there should be nothing extraneous around it. The best way to turn this gig into a nightmare was for one of the guests to scoop up access to the host's home in their soup. She pulled out her apron then dropped her bags on the floor in a corner. She found cleaning wipes and ran one over all the surface areas, although the place was clean enough to eat off the floors. Better safe than sorry.

"Ruth!" Zoey exclaimed to the empty apartment, rushing back to the closet and retrieving her phone from her coat. After turning it on, she saw that her husband had called several more times. She quickly texted an "All good, see you tonight" to her sister and powered the phone back down. Double-checking that her apron was tied tight, she got to work.

Once all the vegetables were cut and the shrimp shelled, cut, and cleaned, Zoey made up the salad and set it in the adjoining fridge to chill without exposing it to any fish smell. The other fridge looked like a typical bachelor refrigerator, filled mostly with bottled water, beer, and several take-out containers. There was more than enough room.

She set the soup stock to simmer and went to see about how to set the table. Zoey left the kitchen in search of the dining room and the fine china through another swinging door on the opposite side of the kitchen.

The dining room table was already set, complete with sorbet dishes at the top of each place setting and a gorgeous centerpiece of fresh flowers.

Did Tristan Malloy do all this himself or had someone lent a feminine touch? Zoey gathered up the sorbet bowls and salad plates, taking them back to the kitchen. Then, with curiosity getting the best of her and a little time to kill, she set off to investigate the apartment. He had told her to make herself at home, after all.

Tristan's apartment held more secrets than clues. Zoey meandered from room to room and down the halls. There wasn't much furniture, save the basics. A large couch and several chairs in the living room. The elegant dining room set that could accommodate twelve, given the extra chairs pushed up against the walls. All the floors, be they marble or wood, were polished and bare. Was she dealing with a germophobe, perhaps?

But all the walls had artwork. Exquisite works, museum caliber.

She opened up the first closed door and her breath came out in a giant rush. It was a library full of books. Shelves that went from the floor to the ten-foot ceiling of all four walls were lined up with books. Hardcovers, paperbacks, classics as well as reference volumes. She couldn't resist running her fingertips along them until she made her way across the room. Not a speck of dust.

In the center, a large oak desk and leather chair. On one corner of the desk was a Mac desktop computer. Next to the computer, the archaic fax machine. Zoey smiled. Tristan Malloy was an enigma wrapped inside a riddle with a side of time warp.

There were three bedrooms with nothing in them except more paintings and large leather benches that she assumed were to sit on to admire the art, like a museum. When she came to the last room, the farthest down the hall, she felt her conscience give a tug. She was going to take a peek into his most personal space, his sanctuary. She should be ashamed, she thought as she opened the door. The first thing Zoey noticed was the familiar smell of what she best remembered her grandfather for . . . Old Spice cologne.

Who is this guy, and why do I even care?

His bedroom, like all the others, was stark but masculine. A king-size bed with a geometric-patterned black comforter and crisp white sheets. A table next to the bed served as a nightstand. There wasn't a dresser, but she could see the open door that led to his walk-in closet. She took several steps toward his bathroom when she spied the gorgeous sunken tub and stopped. This was wrong. If you're doing something that would embarrass the hell out of you should you get caught, then you shouldn't be doing it. This would certainly qualify. Zoey closed the door and swiftly made her way back to the kitchen.

But there was one other thing she noticed. Unless it was hidden in a wall somewhere, there wasn't a single television set. After seeing the number of books in his library, it made sense. But with the exception of the kitchen, the apartment was far from cozy.

The kitchen was where she stayed and where Tristan found her when he returned promptly at five fifteen.

"This place smells heavenly," he announced when he came through the door. She was in full swing, with pots on the stove and the oven working. She wondered which smell was tantalizing him. And whether the tint on his cheeks and forehead was from sun or windburn.

"How was your game?" Zoey asked, like she had a clue about any of it. She knew nothing about the sport and hoped her simple inquiry wasn't taken as an invitation to engage in a full-fledged conversation on the topic.

"I double-bogeyed four holes. Not one of my best rounds."

"Sounds like you were attacked by the bogeyman." *I'll be here all night, folks. Don't forget to tip your waiters.*

Tristan looked at her and deadpanned for a beat before shaking his head. "I think you mean *boogie*."

"Why? Was he dancing?"

"That's very funny."

Clearly it wasn't all that clever and he was just being polite. They stood in awkward silence for a minute until Zoey lifted the lid of the nearest pot and stirred it to look busy.

"If you don't need me for anything, I'm going to go shower and dress for dinner," he said.

It sounded vaguely like he was asking for permission. It was the strangest thing. He had this way of making her feel like she was a guest that he was hosting and not the hired help. She was more accustomed to being ordered around. And she was loath to admit, she was way more interested than she should be in what he looked like cleaned up.

When he returned nearly an hour later, she got her answer.

Chapter 3

If Zoey had to choose a single word to describe Tristan, it would've been *geek*.

She had assumed that a man living on the Upper East Side would be dressing in a suit and tie for a dinner party. Tristan was wearing khaki pants, complete with pleats and relaxed fit, the outline of his suspenders stopping at the trousers' high waist, a white shirt, and a red sweater vest. He topped it all off with a bow tie that had musical notes on it. The only things missing were a pocket protector and a pair of glasses being held together with tape. His hair was still damp and slicked back but devoid of any gel or product.

He was the cutest Brainiac she'd ever laid eyes on.

"Can I borrow an oven for a few minutes?" he asked while going to the fridge and pulling out what she had also wrongly assumed were the take-out containers. "After we got everything all settled, I forgot that an appetizer might be nice, so I whipped up some boudin balls."

"Sure." Zoey walked over to the double ovens, turning the bottom one on to preheat. "I'm only using one. And I must say I'm impressed."

"Don't be. I tried stuffing them with pepper jack cheese. They could be a disaster."

"Do you want me to try to get a quick dipping sauce going?"

"No need." He held up the other container. "I made a pepper jelly."

Tristan pulled out a cookie sheet and started spreading the balls out on it, then halted.

"Do you think it's too much pepper?" he asked, looking truly concerned.

Zoey scrunched up her face. Should she be honest or just placate him? It was too late to do anything about it now. "I'm not sure. I haven't tried it. On a positive note, if it burns out their taste buds, my job got a whole lot easier. They'll never notice if I made a mistake."

"Pitchers of water," he said, settling on a solution. "We need pitchers of water."

"Already done. There's one in the fridge and one

on the wet bar. And if anyone complains, you can just blame me."

Tristan visibly relaxed. "I would never do that to you, but I can't thank you enough for offering."

"We're in this thing together."

Zoey would've never been able to answer why she was considering them a team. It was not how these things usually went down. She had been told on more than one occasion the new Golden Rule—he who holds the gold makes the rules. Her services were a luxury, not a necessity. Every time she stood her ground, she ran the risk of losing a repeat customer. Positive word of mouth was crucial. But Tristan Malloy was different. She wanted to help him.

"If you want me to, I can taste one before I bring them out. If they don't work out, I'll just start serving a little sooner," she said from her side of the island. That was another thing she noticed—he kept a healthy distance between them at all times. He didn't overcrowd or overstep. "Now why don't you throw those things in the oven and go pour yourself a glass of either water or wine and get ready to greet your guests?"

"Thanks, Zoey. You're a lifesaver. This is my first time doing this. I think I'm a little nervous."

"With a kitchen like this? You should be entertaining all the time."

"I love to cook," he admitted, "but I normally only do it for myself. And I don't know that I'd classify this as entertaining. It's more of a business meeting. I don't have many, but the ones I do have are held in stuffy offices and crowded restaurants. They make me antsy. I don't think I'm a very good city person."

"Are you obsessive-compulsive when it comes to germs?" Zoey blurted. They had lapsed into relaxed conversation. That might have been a tad too personal. She was a cook, not a therapist. "I mean, the whole place is spotless. The floors look clean enough to eat off of."

He seemed to genuinely consider it. "I don't think so. I just came from a very different upbringing. Moving to New York was one of those things I did jumping in with both feet. But here I am, almost two years later, and I still haven't embraced the life."

"It's a huge culture shock. I'm from Cleveland and I'm still trying to adjust to the difference."

"How long have you lived here?"

"About ten months. I'm starting to get the feeling that you either love it or hate it immediately."

"You may be onto something there."

Zoey would've loved to engage him more, get the full backstory, and find out why his home was more like an art gallery. But they were interrupted by his intercom buzzing. His guests had begun to arrive.

"It's officially showtime. Don't worry about a thing. I've got your back."

She gave him a reassuring smile and he gave her a nod of his head and left the kitchen. The next thing she heard was music beating softly out of the speakers above her head. Jazz. A little mood music.

"Nice touch, Mr. Malloy," she softly mused.

The first thing Zoey did was taste the sauce and add a bit of fresh squeezed lemon juice to it to tame the pepper flavor before warming it. It did the trick. When she quietly slid into the living room to place the plated tray on the bar where the party of six other men and one woman were gathered, Tristan was the first to grab one of the appetizers by the toothpick she had inserted in each of the boudin balls, dunk it in the sauce, and eat it. His eyebrows rose and he gave her a covert wink. She had saved his balls, and he knew it. She snickered to herself when safely back in the kitchen.

The men were all dressed in the usual corporate attire, suit and tie. The woman, a sleeveless navy-blue dress. Zoey gave a silent prayer of thanks for being able to break away from convention and having to wear the dreaded sleeveless dress, a garment that had to have been designed by men, to make sure that ladies worked overtime at the gym. Not only did it leave even the most secure woman running the risk of "bat wing" if she so much as extended her arm, but men got to wear jackets to hide their sweat stains, while women got to freeze in the winter to accommodate the style. At least Tristan was the grand equalizer, dressed casually enough to make any guest feel comfortable.

They worked in unison the entire night. Zoey plated the salad and left it for him, taking the soup bowls back with her into the kitchen. Within minutes, Tristan was moving the party into the dining room.

The evening would have been borderline as magical, save for one thing. As a professional, Zoey had to take into consideration the kind of event she was working and have her own behavior reflect that. The Turkish guys wanted to talk to her the entire time. A kid's party was more her wisecracking while serving them. This particular situation called for her to remain as unobtrusive as possible. And she was.

She wouldn't admit to herself that she was trying to glean information about Tristan while she moved about the room, serving and cleaning. But she couldn't get anything that she would define as helpful. Mostly because everyone else in the room would take note of her presence and promptly clam up. They seemed to resent her being there. Every glance she made in Tristan's direction revealed little more than that he didn't care if the rest of the party were uncomfortable. Whenever she entered to serve or quickly clear, the conversation would all but stop. The silence was strained, before someone would bring up the weather or where they had just been on vacation. Once she made eye contact with him and he gave her the smallest hint of a smirk. But the other times, he just let the members of his party sit there awkwardly fiddling with their forks or taking a sip of water and looked from one to the other, bemused. They seemed to tolerate it. None of the people acknowledged her when she cleared anything away from them. Tristan was the only one to thank her, and he did it for everything.

Except for one time, while she was serving dessert. Zoey had already made up her mind that she would do the final cleanup after all the guests had left. They had made it abundantly clear she wasn't welcome. She knew how to take a hint. There was plenty to keep her busy. She tried to wash things as she used them, but there was still plenty of suds-dunking to do after it was over, no matter how big a dishwasher. When she brought out the little dishes of bread pudding with a scoop of fresh whipped cream infused with vanilla, the only woman in the group was in the middle of a sentence. Something about encrypting fees. Innocuous really, she was quoting something in *Forbes,* so it couldn't have been classified material.

"I think what she's trying to say is, she keeps up with current events. While on *vacation*. Where was it you went last month? Hawaii?" One of the men spoke up, shifting his eyes quickly to Zoey and then back to the woman, who stopped talking and now had pink tingeing her cheeks.

Zoey could also feel the heat start to rise. The guy she had pegged as the ringleader of the group had completed the classic slam dunk. With only the condescending tone of his voice, he was trying to put the woman in her place. And he was trying to make every man at the table take a moment to picture the attractive young blonde in a bikini. Zoey tried to place the dishes as fast as she could before she misbehaved and ruined Tristan's whole evening.

"The truth of the matter is—" the man went on.

Then she heard Tristan's voice.

"Doug, I'd like to let Kristin finish her thought. She makes a valid point. I read the article as well, and I agree with what she's said so far."

Zoey finished placing the dishes in the much more familiar silence. She beat it out of there to the safety of the kitchen. But she had to give props to Tristan for having the woman's back.

She loaded the dishwasher, digging the jazz and thinking about how she was having way too much fun tonight. She played around a spectacular kitchen with all the freshest ingredients she didn't have to buy. And the man footing the bill seemed like a genuinely nice guy. By midnight she'd be leaving the ball and her fairy tale would come to an end. And because she had been able to bite her tongue, maybe one of those bozos would want to throw a gig her way.

The party broke up soon after. It wasn't long before he was pushing through the swinging door to the kitchen and found her up to her elbows in sudsy water.

"You don't have to do this," he began earnestly.

"Sure, I do. It's part of the service," she replied. "I leave the place exactly as I found it."

"I'm certainly getting my money's worth. And everything was delicious. You did a great job tonight, Zoey, thank you. And I see you didn't bring a server."

"Don't worry"—she gave a relaxed laugh—"you still got billed for one. And normally I wouldn't be so candid, but it was the right call. I don't think your guests appreciated me being there. One more person serving would've made conversation next to impossible."

Tristan pulled a dish towel out of a drawer before closing it with a hip check. He leaned against the counter, still keeping to his side of the room. His eyes were downcast so that she couldn't see them. But his voice had a ring of boyish guilt.

"Since we're being honest, I have a confession to make. And an apology. I used you as a decoy of sorts."

Zoey wasn't sure what her correct reaction should be. "You did?"

"I'm the inventor of a computer software program that compiles data. Lots of it. It's able to pull it out of multiple sources and combine them. I realized after I sold it, in the wrong hands, it's capable of doing great harm. People who always want to meet in crowded restaurants have the ability to communicate with each other with their target unable to hear everything they say over the noise. I don't want any distractions when I'm conducting business. And who doesn't like a home field advantage, right? I had a hunch that I could also use an extra pair of eyes and ears in the room. You can tell a lot about people by how they behave toward those that have nothing to offer them."

"Sort of like, you can tell a lot about a person's character by how they treat the waitstaff?"

He looked like he might apologize again. Zoey wasn't referring to the rude indifference of the guests who had just left; that was nothing more than an uncomfortable annoyance. Turned out, he was angry on her behalf.

"I really take offense to men disrespecting women. Women are the original multitaskers, and men know it. I think strong women make them nervous, so they resort to the only thing they can fall back on—brute force. Where is the honor in that?"

"I'd be lying if I didn't say how much I enjoyed you sticking it to that one guy."

"My grandfather used to say, 'Being male is a matter of birth. Being a man is a matter of age. Being a gentleman is a matter of choice.'"

"That's pretty profound."

"Isn't that what all grandparents are supposed to be? Full of wisdom and life experience?"

"Yes, but I think people forget that these days. Or just don't care enough to take the time to listen. My grandmother spent her last years telling us to stick her on a block of ice and set her adrift."

"She wanted to die alone?"

"Nah, we think she just had a thing for Eskimo folklore."

They shared a chuckle before his face got serious again. "In this particular instance though, I took their silence whenever you came into the room as them having to keep their guard up. Everyone who approaches me knows I can't sell them the original program. It belongs to the government. And when you work with the government, they don't take kindly to you working for anyone else. Corporate bigwigs get through the door under the guise of wanting something similar, but it usually ends up the same—they want me to do something that's not only morally wrong, but also could get me sent to prison. I get when the government acts all secretive, but these people were from a pharmaceutical company. I seriously doubt they were worried about you finding out where they stash the erythromycin. My guess is that they wanted to find a way to circumvent HIPAA guidelines."

He had such great wit for someone with an expert poker face. The combination was most likely dangerous as hell, but he was too noble to utilize it.

"I figured, if you were treated like an interloper, chances are the people that want the program had something to hide. You never said one word to them. For all they knew, you didn't even know English."

"You're right! I was quiet the whole night. Looks like your sketchy meter was spot-on."

His face clouded over with what she could only describe as melancholy. "I'm not always the best judge of character. I shouldn't even be entertaining these requests."

"You could've fooled me."

"I'm a little too trusting. I do much better when I can observe as an outsider."

He had begun taking pots and pans to dry and put away as Zoey washed them. It reminded her of home when she was a kid. Ruth and Zoey would take turns washing when they were little. Once Ruth started painting her nails and bedazzling them with artwork, she only wanted to dry. Not long after that, the chore was handed down to their younger siblings and they were put on laundry detail.

"Where are you from?" Zoey asked, enjoying the company and the conversation.

"Born in Rhode Island, but did most of my growing up in the Virgin Islands."

"That's a pretty big switch."

Tristan paused. "Okay, so this is the part where I'm going to make you unnecessarily uncomfortable. My parents died when I was three."

"I'm so sorry," Zoey said.

"It's all right. Seriously. I barely remember them. Dense fog, drunk driver, they were together and it was quick, which is the best anyone can hope for when you think about it. My grandfather was retired military. Loved golf. My grandmother was a dedicated army wife who loved to entertain. Both hated the cold. They bought and ran a small resort right near a golf course in St. Croix. A glorified bed-and-breakfast, if you will.

Most of our guests were cronies of my grandfather and their wives. It was quiet, peaceful. I spent my whole young life barefoot, learning golf, and helping maintain the property. My grandparents thought they had really made the leap into the twenty-first century when they got dial-up Internet. They would let me have access to it, but it's not like I could do much. One time I tried to play a game online, I think it was Sonic the Hedgehog, and the thing froze for hours. My grandparents were so uninterested, they didn't even notice."

His explanation solved the mystery of why he seemed stuck in a time warp of manners, courtesy, and pleated pants. "I can see why after two years in New York, you still feel like a deer getting caught in the headlights."

"Am I that obvious?"

She couldn't tell if his behavior was that noticeable or she was just tuned into him. She felt the same level of protective instinct that she felt for her younger siblings. What Tristan Malloy had in years, he lacked in experience.

"I wouldn't have guessed if you hadn't told me," she answered honestly.

They kept washing and drying the dishes together, quietly enjoying the smooth jazz still playing from the surround-sound speakers.

"How did you end up here?" Zoey asked.

Tristan put his dish towel down, crossing his arms over his chest, a faraway look taking over. He didn't appear put off talking about it, but more like he wanted to get the chronological order of events correct.

"One of the regulars at Paradise Cove was a retired lieutenant colonel who was working for a government contractor. He was a good guy, loved to talk about technology. By the time I was sixteen, my grandmother made the announcement that I was done with home-schooling. After that I spent all my spare time trying to figure out everything I could about that computer with its dial-up, how to make it work better, faster."

"Ambitious little cuss, weren't you?"

He preened a little. "I like to think so. Long story short, with some help from the colonel, I devised a program that links databases. The colonel took it to his former superiors and they bought it for what I consider an outrageous sum of money. The program renews every year with a few updates. Now I spend a half hour every year striking a few keys on the keyboard and collect my check."

In no way did it sound like he was bragging, merely answering the question. She was dying to know what he considered an outrageous sum of money but knew that was a question she didn't deserve the answer to.

"So you decided to take on the Big Apple?" Zoey asked instead.

"Not originally. I would've been more than happy to stay on the island, totally remodel Paradise Cove, and hire a full staff so that my grandparents could retire in style, but I didn't get that chance."

He sounded melancholy again, and Zoey bit into her lower lip in response to it.

"They died, didn't they?"

He nodded.

"I'm sorry I brought it up."

"It's okay, Zoey. Not talking about it doesn't change anything. My grandmother died first, after a relatively short bout with Alzheimer's. A blessing really, when you think about how long that agony can go on. My grandfather and I took care of her ourselves, with some help of course. He didn't last six months after she was gone. It's strange, when he was in the army, he would be gone for months at a time. I guess as long as he knew she was waiting for him to return, he could take it. After she was gone, he just gave up."

Zoey gave him a consoling pat on his shoulder. "I'm so sorry, Tristan."

He didn't recoil from her touch, but within seconds, he was back on his side of the room, grabbing a beer out of the fridge.

"Thanks, Zoey," he said, before twisting off the top and taking a long swig. "After they were gone, all I knew was I needed to get away. From the resort, from the island. I had heard, and overheard, so many stories about the mainland over the years. In a moment of grief and determination, I decided on New York."

He didn't sound like he was proud of his accomplishment. He hadn't embraced city life; he endured it. The evening was turning from a success to a downer, and that was the last thing she wanted. She turned off the water, squeezed the sponge one last time, and put it back in its hiding place.

"What made you decide on Cajun tonight?" she asked to change the subject.

He gave her a small grin. "I've never been to New Orleans."

Was he telling the truth or did he feel like he had exposed himself enough? Zoey took the dish towel he'd left on the counter and started wiping down the already clean counters, aware that he was watching her as she did so. She surveyed the room to make sure that everything was put away and clean, then added, "This is the most beautiful kitchen I've ever had the enjoyment of working in."

He smiled again, this time relaxed and real. "Thanks. You did a great job tonight. All the way around."

"It's easy in a setup like this."

He reached into his pocket and handed her a wad of cash she didn't bother to count. This man was not ripping her off. "Would you rather get paid by check?"

"Heck no! Not only is cash king, but it's virtually untraceable by the IRS. It's called—getting paid under the table."

"What table is that?" he inquired.

Zoey threw her hands up in the air with a shrug. "Beats me. Maybe the table you would write the check on?"

"Can I call on you again?"

"Certainly," Zoey said quickly, already looking forward to the prospect of working for him again. "And if you don't mind spreading the good word, I'd sure appreciate it. Word of mouth is great for advertising in this business."

He paused before picking up her faded doctor's bag and handing it to her with a reluctant "Sure."

They walked together to the front door, where he helped her with her coat and she gathered the rest of her things. "Can I call you a cab?"

"Nope. I'm all good," she said as he opened the door. "Thanks again, Tristan. It's been a pleasure."

"I assure you, Zoey, the pleasure was all mine. Good night."

He closed the door and Zoey started back down the long hall. It was her turn to feel an indescribable sadness. Tristan Malloy had been the dream client, so kind and accommodating. Then she pushed the down arrow elevator button and reached into her pocket to count the money he gave her.

That's when she realized she still had his spare key in her pocket.

Chapter 4

Zoey was annoyed. She prided herself on her attention to detail. She trudged back down the hallway to his door, weary from a night on her feet. She gave a knock. After waiting a minute and not getting an answer, she knocked again, harder. Loud enough that it resounded through the empty hall. Again, she waited.

"Odd," she mumbled under her breath, pulling out her phone and finding his number. She waited for it to ring ten times before disconnecting. It didn't forward to voice mail.

She stood outside Tristan Malloy's door and slowly built up the steam that ended in her mind completely running away with her. She had just left him not five minutes ago. What the hell could've happened to him?

She stared at her phone, silently begging the screen to light up with his callback to no avail. Panic mounted with indecision and she pounded on the door, then pushed the tiny button that was supposed to act as a doorbell, then gave up. She stuck the key in the lock.

She swung open the door and then froze.

Aerosmith?

Gone was the jazz music. The whole apartment throbbed with Steven Tyler screaming the lyrics to "Walk This Way."

"Tristan?" she called out, knowing her voice wasn't much above a whisper, given the level of the sound system. The only response she got was a droning, blasting demand for her to keep putting one foot in front of the other and continue.

It was hypnotic, commanding. She began the systematic search of the apartment, similar to the investigation she had made earlier, but with quick glances. The rooms she had looked in earlier were all still empty. When she approached the open door to his bedroom, her skin prickled with anticipation and sweat broke out on her upper lip.

She stopped short as soon as she caught the first glimpse of his reflection in his bathroom mirror.

Gone were the bow tie, sweater vest, and perfectly pressed khakis. His dress shirt was still on, unbuttoned and shirttail pulled out, covering the top of the black leather pants he was now wearing. They weren't skin-tight, but as he shook his hips and moved his feet and arms with the music, the white shirt rose and fell. There was no mistaking . . . hiding under that hanging crisp white cotton was an extraordinary pair of buns. His chest was broad, her first impression of seeing his abs in his golf shirt now confirmed. His hair was flying free in playful disarray, the ends damp with sweat. And man could he dance, better than any boy band rock star she ever crushed on. He was singing into a panto-mimed microphone, which looked only slightly less silly than if he were improvising with a hairbrush. The song went into the next verse, and he could've won a lip sync battle. He had all the moves and the muscles to match. Lean, tight, flexible.

"Holy cannoli," she breathed as she continued to spy on him while he cut loose. This was a complete de-parture from the man she had been with all day. Now all she could think of was—this dancing machine had no business being kept hidden from the world. When he belted out the line about giving him a kiss, she was tempted.

He stopped the action the moment he caught sight of her shadow in the mirror, accompanied by an actual mic-drop. He swiveled quickly, coming face-to-face with her, still standing a few feet away in his bedroom. They were both embarrassed, but for different reasons. He rushed past her to turn down the volume control knob on the wall in his room. She caught a whiff of leather mixed with sweat and the last remnants of Old Spice.

"Zoey," he said, making a concerted effort to sound steady while trying to catch his breath. "I wasn't expecting you."

Despite her legitimately having broken into his home, he still couldn't stop being polite.

"I forgot to give you back your key," Zoey stammered. She held out her hand to show it to him, unable to take her wide eyes off his mostly bare chest as the shirt opened wider. "I tried knocking. And calling. But I guess you didn't hear it over the Aerosmith."

Tristan cast his eyes downward, noticed the state of his shirt, and grabbed both sides of it to close the gap. "Sorry."

Zoey wasn't sure if the apology was meant for missing her knocking or for the unexpected peep show. "I was going to leave it on the kitchen counter, but, you know, I was just doing what Steven Tyler told me to."

"Yeah, I get that," he replied, concentrating on his fingers fumbling to get his shirt buttoned back up. "He's very persuasive."

The trance of seeing him in all the skin and leather-clad glory began to wane, replaced with an irrational anger. Forget that Zoey had stumbled upon him un-invited in the privacy of his own bathroom and his first response was an apology. Forget that in reality they were little more than strangers. Her head was spinning with a hundred questions. On the top of that list—just what kind of game was Tristan Malloy playing?

"When you didn't answer, I was worried something happened to you," she told him, her voice registering ir-ritation. "I'm not sure if I still should be. Nice pants."

"I bought them online," he said sheepishly. "I think they're too big."

"You're supposed to buy them a size smaller than you would normally wear, because they stretch. And most people go to a store and try them on." What she was really thinking was, if they were any tighter, she may have had a stroke. Then she mentally cursed herself for not checking out his closet, since it was ob-viously where he kept his secrets. "Getting in touch with your wild side, were you?"

Tristan looked down again at his white sock–wearing feet and shuffled from one of them to the other before saying sheepishly, "It's how I let go of stress. By pre-tending I'm a rock star."

He sounded so contrite, when he had every reason to be mad. He was perfectly within his rights to tell her off. The lost boy was back. Zoey's ire evaporated. "I didn't know you were stressed. I thought the evening went very well."

Not yet brave enough to meet her gaze, he went over to the corner of his bed and sat down, running a hand through his hair. "It did, as far as the food was concerned at any rate. But like I told you, I'm terrible in social situations."

Zoey let out a heavy sigh before going over to sit beside him, their legs nearly touching. "You seemed so relaxed with those people. I had no idea."

He finally looked at her. "You're right. You really don't."

"Do you want to talk about it?"

She watched the emotions play across his face. He was debating whether or not he wanted to open up. If he could trust her.

"You'll think I'm an idiot."

"Probably," she said. "But that doesn't mean you won't feel better unloading. I already think you have a freaky Jekyll-and-Hyde thing going on."

They exchanged small smiles, and the tension started to ease.

"Remember me mentioning I'm a terrible judge of character?"

"Of course." She remembered the entire night from start to finish.

"My first stop in the States after my grandfather died wasn't New York. It was Las Vegas."

"You wanted to move there?"

"I was considering it. I thought it would be warm, which I was used to. I didn't think it would be as hot as it was. There's no ocean breezes in the desert. But I had heard it was amazing there, full of every sight and sound imaginable. I didn't care all that much about gambling. There are casinos back home, though I could count on one hand the times I had been to them. But I had money to burn and wasn't opposed to it either. I booked myself a fancy room at a ritzy hotel for an extended stay. I figured I'd take a little time to live the high life and splurge myself out of my grief."

He paused. They sat alone together in silence until Zoey reached out, placing her hand on the butter-soft leather covering his leg. "That's hardly a crime, Tristan. Even if you lost a fortune, it was yours to lose."

"Agreed. But I don't know, I didn't expect so many people being rude and drunk and inappropriate. And everyone seemed to be with groups of other people they knew. Bachelor parties and brides wearing sashes and tiaras, all partying with their friends, having a blast. Extended families on vacations and reunions. Stuff I watched from the safety of a slot machine. I was in the adult entertainment capital of the world, and within two days I felt like I was alone on Mars."

He began to frown. Zoey got it. It was a feeling she knew well.

"That night I went to the bar to have a nightcap. That's when I met Veronica. She was beautiful, effervescent, friendly. I got up the nerve to nod in her direction and she struck up a conversation. Next thing I knew, I was buying her a drink and we ended up talking the rest of the night away. We started meeting every night at the bar, around the same time. We talked about deep and meaningful subjects. It was like she was reading my mind most of the time. I really felt a connection with her. I was smitten even before she turned on the flirting and touching."

Zoey thought she would save him and cut directly to the chase. "Let me guess, she was a gold digger who took you for everything you had?"

He gave a pained shake of his head. "Not everything. Just the thousand dollars she said I owed her."

"Oh, my God." She raised a quick hand and added a cough to mask the laugh that escaped before adding, "She was a hooker."

This time Tristan nodded. "She used the term *call girl,* which is kind of ironic, since I never got her phone number."

"You knew prostitution is legal in Vegas, right?" Zoey felt so sorry for him.

"Yeah, but I thought you had to go to an actual bordello. It felt so natural being with her. When she suggested going back to my room to have sex, I couldn't get her out of the bar fast enough. The whole elevator ride she was all over me. I thought I was the luckiest guy alive."

"She didn't make herself clear?" Zoey asked in disbelief. "Isn't there some sort of protocol for those things? Like, don't you have to agree to the price or something?"

He shrugged before returning all his concentration to his sock-covered big toe. "She may have, I don't remember. I already felt guilty for having sex without any emotional commitment. As soon as it was over, she started putting her clothes back on. To lighten the blow, she told me she was giving me her discount rate because she had genuinely enjoyed talking to me. To say I was humiliated is an understatement."

"So why did you pay her? You could've told her to get lost." Zoey asked the question despite knowing the answer. He was a gentleman who sounded like he spent his young life taking orders like a good soldier.

"I was so mortified by my own stupidity, I just wanted to get her out of there. It was a small price to pay. What if she called the cops or made a scene? I would've died on the spot. And I've read stories about pimps. I don't know if she had one, but I wasn't willing to take the chance of finding out."

"I forgot about them. Yeah, you did the right thing." She wanted desperately to say something that would wipe the self-recrimination off his face.

"We used a condom, but I walked around for a year waiting to drop dead from some disease before I went to a doctor here in Manhattan and confessed. The only saving grace was what a nonissue the whole episode was to him. He told me with what he'd seen over his career, on a scale of one to ten, my story was a two."

"You checked out okay, right?"

"I'm fine." He tried to smile and shrugged again. "Still a pretty pathetic way to have your first sexual encounter."

Oh, hell *no!* Zoey's inner voice shouted. He was too nice a guy to have been dissed and dismissed in such a fashion. Did guys value their virginity the same way girls were supposed to? It didn't matter what the correct answer was. She hadn't known Tristan long, but she was sure he valued his.

"Almost everybody's first time is a train wreck. You are not alone in that." It was the best she could come up with. "So, what happened next?"

"Isn't all that bad enough?" Tristan's chuckle had a ring of a weight being lifted off his shoulders.

"It is!" Zoey laughed in agreement. "But you might as well finish the story of how you got here."

"I stayed in that hotel room, in the dark, for a week. I didn't get out of bed. The thought of running into her again made me want to throw up. The next time I left that room was when I checked out of the hotel. I took a cab to the airport, decided on going to New York, and that was it."

There were still scads of questions Zoey wanted to ask, but it was hard to broach the topics without revealing that she had scoped out his place while he was gone. Luckily, she didn't have to.

"I had all these great visions in my mind of how I would blend in with the scenery here. I could play golf after a short ride in almost any direction. I could visit museums and enjoy fine dining. But I couldn't shake what had happened in Vegas and felt like an enormous loser. That made it next to impossible to make any real connections, let alone friends. Eating alone in public all the time left me feeling like more of a misfit. Even in the public library, I thought I could hear people laughing at me. I had my first panic attack in the Metropolitan Museum of Art."

Hard to remain impassive when a man looks like he's about to cry. This poor guy couldn't seem to catch a break, no matter how luxurious his surroundings. "So you turned your home into a museum."

If he had realized she had given herself away as a snoop, he didn't let on. "It didn't start out that way. It started out with the purchase of a few lithographs of famous works. Then I got up the nerve to venture out to art auctions, where all I had to do was hold up a little paddle. Once word spread that I had money, sellers came to me. Before long, I had my own collection. I had the kitchen remodeled so that I could cook for myself, something I always enjoyed doing with Grandma at the Cove. Golf supplies the fresh air and exercise, but I can do it by myself. I spend the rest of my time cleaning this place and trying to fend off people like the group you met tonight."

"Did it put an end to the panic attacks?"

"It did. Only now I'm afraid I'm not just awkward, I'm paralyzed."

There are times in one's life where you reach a crossroads. When your only options are to stay in your comfort zone or take a leap of faith. Zoey had taken that leap when she came to New York, and while it wasn't all rainbows and unicorns, it was a million times better than what she had left behind. Tristan had already proved he could take care of himself. Now he just needed to enjoy life. He deserved it as much as she did. The things they held in common vastly out-numbered their differences. The words tumbled forth from her mouth.

"Tristan, I'd like to think you consider me a friend. And it looks like you could sure use one. I think I can help you, if you'd let me."

Chapter 5

When Zoey returned to her own apartment, it was well past midnight. Tristan insisted his car service drive her home. She'd spent most of that ride devising a plan that she could implement without overwhelming him. She wasn't a psychiatrist, she was a kindred spirit, after all. If she went too fast it could make matters worse for the gentle loner. It would be a tragedy to end up leaving him so jaded, he would spend the rest of his life a bitter man. Kind, respectful men were a hot commodity, and he just needed to add a little self-esteem to be quite a catch. He had willingly put his trust in her, and she didn't want to fail him.

The driver who picked her up gave her a quiet hello and nothing more. The company likely had the instructions that the rides from this address had a "no interaction" policy.

From the safety of the Lincoln Town Car and its silent, focused driver, she pulled the money Tristan gave her out of her pocket and counted it. Tristan had given her double her price quote, a 100 percent tip. She had to toughen him up, or the city would eat him alive.

Ruth was on the futon in the living room, waiting for her, wearing pajamas decorated with cows jumping over moons, the television on for background noise.

"I was starting to worry about you," she said, looking up from the magazine in her lap.

"I can't believe you're home," Zoey replied. She tossed her bags in their designated spot. "Aren't you supposed to be up to your ice cubes in Thirsty Thursday?"

"I was out, but when I texted you and you didn't answer me, I cut the night short."

"Sorry." Zoey pulled her phone out of her coat pocket, turning it back on. "I forgot I had it off. I didn't want to be disturbed while working."

"You mean you didn't want to deal with Derek. How did the job go?"

Before Zoey could recap the evening, her phone started to ring.

"Speak of the devil." Ruth smirked.

Zoey rolled her eyes and answered the call. She headed to the bedroom for some privacy.

"I'm not finished with you yet!" Ruth called out. Zoey gave a backward wave while still moving.

"Hello?" Zoey said, closing the bedroom door behind her.

"Where were you so late?"

She saw no point in playing dumb.

"Derek, if this is supposed to be a friendly call, you're going about it the wrong way. And if it's the beginning of an interrogation, you're on the fast track to me hanging up."

"I'm sorry." He instantly scaled back the heavy handedness. "But I don't think you know how much I worry about you up there."

"That's nice, but I'm a big girl. And I don't see you showing the same level of concern for my sister."

"That's because she's not my wife. And Ruthless can take care of herself."

Zoey's jaw began to clench. "You know what? I have always hated the little pet name you have for my sister, no matter how amusing she may think it is. Now how did you get this number and why exactly are you calling me at this hour?"

"I gave up my job at the club," Derek said, ignoring her question.

"Gave up or got fired?"

"I quit. I gave up drinking too. Got a real respectable job installing drywall."

"And just how long are you planning to stay in the glamorous world of spackling?"

She could hear him starting to tense up. "I'm also working on getting my real estate license. So why don't you stop all of this foolishness and come home?"

"Because we agreed on a year's separation."

"I don't need a year to know you belong with me. You wanted me to change. I've done everything you asked."

Even if Zoey wanted to believe him, she'd still have doubts. She'd put in hours of overtime waitressing for four years as he drifted from job to job, never lasting for more than six months. Except for bouncing at a nightclub in town. Once he passed the six-month mark, Zoey knew it was a job he enjoyed, which made her uneasy. Derek always found time to get to the gym, something she never managed, with all the running around she did. He had the stature to see above a crowd and liked to exude authority. Not only did the job mess up both their schedules, but he would also bring home that air of aggressiveness and reeked of booze and stale cigarette smoke. That made it easy for Zoey to keep her distance. It also taught her just how comfortable a big bed was for sleeping alone.

"I've heard all this before, Derek."

"Where were you tonight?" His voice started to rise. "Are you seeing someone?"

The accusations were more like it, and what she was used to when he didn't get his way. "I was *working*. You didn't mind the late hours when you were sitting on the couch, drinking beer, placing profiles on OkCupid. And random hookups were more your style."

"Damnit, Zoey! We can't move forward if you keep bringing up the past!"

And with that, she hung up.

Their marriage hadn't started out that way. Her high school sweetheart, Derek, would talk about all he wanted them to do, all he wanted to be. When he had gotten down on one knee and asked her to hold out her hand, he had promised her adventures and traveling and discovery, not to mention a lifetime of love and security. She left the tiny diamond ring behind when she took off. She was tired of feeling owned.

They shared dreams and aspirations while she cooked for him in their tiny kitchen, giggling and teasing the whole time. Derek's transformation to sullen and moody was so gradual, she'd hardly noticed. It wasn't until she detected the familiar alcohol on his breath early in the afternoon that she was forced to acknowledge the honeymoon was over. How she hated that smell.

They stopped going out when a subscription to Netflix seemed like a good idea for cozy nights and the ease of an order on Grubhub. They'd stuck a lot of forks in toss-out containers over the last couple years, but his favorite recliner only had room for one. Every time Zoey tried to join him out of romantic spontaneity or just to feel some human contact, the protests from the chair and the man were equal. She got too tired to cook for him, and he began to nitpick and criticize when she did. Then he started working at the nightclub and they were little more than ships passing in the night.

Worst of all was his dogged insistence that they should start a family. It came up each and every time she mentioned trying something new or adventurous. Whether it was trying to find a way to go to culinary school or packing up and moving to a new city, the conversation was always the same. It went from discussion to arguing. Then he would want to make up by wrapping his arms around her in bed and whispering in her ear—"Let's make a baby."

No matter how charming he was, Zoey wasn't buying it. Derek didn't have some deep-rooted longing to be a parent. He wanted to trap her, seal the deal, make it that much harder for her to have any interests she could pursue on her own. He refused to listen when she listed her reasons for wanting to wait. Soon she would be turned off as soon as he said it. Why couldn't he say "make love"? "Get down"? "Do the nasty"?

She stormed in and told him she was leaving while he was at the club. Then she stole her own car out of the parking lot and drove to New York. They hammered out the trial-separation-for-a-year deal from Ruth's apartment, with Ruth playing mediator from a second handset. Derek never lasted more than three days before calling to check up on her. Now he knew she had acquired a cell phone.

Zoey went back out to the living room and flopped down on the futon beside her sister. "Ugh."

"It couldn't have gone that bad," Ruth said. "I didn't hear any screaming."

"Never underestimate the power of the END button."

"You're really going to make him sweat this one out, aren't you?"

"You seem to forget my original intention was not to go back at all. If I had any backbone, this whole thing would already be over."

"You said that when you first got here and were all fed up. Are you really thinking about not going home?"

"Are you tired of me as your roomie?"

"No. But by the way you work and then just hang around here, I figured you were missing him as much as he misses you."

Zoey could've pointed out that she was trying to get a business up and running but didn't want to rehash the same dialogue. Ruth sometimes made her affection for Derek a little too well known. To the point where Zoey sometimes wondered where her sister's loyalty stood. Ruth had been living in New York for years with holiday visits, when everyone was on their best behavior. The Derek Ruth remembered was from back in the day, when they were dating. Zoey would be the first to admit, she missed that Derek too.

"Can we talk about something else?" Zoey asked, pulling off her black sensible shoes and wiggling her toes. Ahhhh.

"We certainly can. How did the ragin' Cajun work out?"

"Hasta la pasta!" Zoey exclaimed, taking her feet off the table and sitting up straight with the energy surge. In the madness of the phone call, she had forgotten. "You are not going to believe this one."

Ruth sat up too, tucking her legs beneath her and reaching for her half glass of white wine. "Oh boy. Did he turn out to be a creeper? Start talking."

"Okay. So, this guy is a transplant from the Virgin Islands. Some techno geek who spends all his time cleaning and playing golf. Completely a fish out of water. Strange apartment that looks more like the MoMA but with a kitchen like something out of a magazine. Food went well, he made the appetizer on his own. He was super nice, paid me double my quote, and went out of his way to stick up for the only other woman who was there."

Zoey stopped short of telling Ruth about the forgotten key and what transpired after.

"You're leaving out the most important detail," Ruth hedged.

"What's that?"

"You know, is he cute?"

Zoey paused to take another moment to recall the abs, the backside, the leather, and the booty shake. "Yeah. But sheltered. Way sheltered."

"Like baby duck cute? Or Adam Levine cute?"

"I don't know! I guess he's the kind of cute Adam Levine would be if he were a baby duck."

"Hmm." Ruth was always too good at reading her. "There's a piece missing here. You didn't get this excited over the Turkish guys. And they all played soccer. Did he end up offering you a job, like you thought he might?"

Zoey couldn't hold back the little smile, remembering the green eyes that registered all that relief before he took her up on her offer. He had asked if they could start tomorrow. She told him she'd meet him in front of his building at noon.

"I wouldn't exactly call it a job. It's more of a project."

Ruth drained her wineglass and narrowed her eyes. "What kind of a project?"

Zoey was being guarded, and she wasn't sure why. Ruth was not only her sister but also her best friend. It was stupid to think she could hide anything from her, and why would she want to? If she was going to nurture a friendship with Tristan, Ruth was eventually going to be in the equation as well.

"This poor dude is really having a hard time getting the most out of city life. He came here not knowing anybody."

Ruth scoffed. "Sounds like somebody I know. And *you* are going to be the one to help him with that?"

"I beg your pardon. I knew you! And I've adapted fine here. Sure, I don't spend my weekends clubbing, but that's more out of respect for Derek and our agreement. I'm not going to cheat on him just for the sake of hooking up." *Even if that's exactly what he thinks I'm doing.*

"Looks like you're lining someone up for when that clock counts down. . . ." If Zoey didn't know better, she would swear she heard some judgment in her sister's tone.

"Seriously, not this guy, even if what you're thinking was true. Which it's not. He's a little skittish, not to mention he dresses like an old man. He just needs a friend."

"I'll be Adam Baby Duck's friend," Ruth offered with her usual vixen grin.

"Oh no." Zoey held her hand up. "No way. You'll eat this poor soul alive. He's not even remotely ready to handle the likes of you."

Ruth stuck out her lower lip in her patented pout. "But you promise to let me know when he is?"

Zoey nodded, thinking that while she may hate the Ruthless nickname that Derek gave her, there were times when it did apply.

Chapter 6

Zoey wasn't the least bit surprised when she turned the corner onto East Seventy-Ninth at 11:55 and Tristan was already standing outside, his back fully pressed up against the building wall. He wasn't wearing his purple windbreaker but a blue, puffy down jacket that he could've put back in the closet a month ago. Spring was just around the corner, but encased in all that coat, he looked like he was ready for an expedition to the polar ice cap. Then she remembered the climate he came from and realized forty-five degrees may, in fact, feel like the tundra to him. Still, she hoped she could get him to try on a little more leather. His hands were jammed into the pockets of his brown corduroys up to the wrist. He kept his head down, only periodically lifting it to glance both ways down the street. Zoey couldn't wait to teach him her city walk. As soon as he saw her, he straightened up to his full height and a toothy smile appeared. The kind of smile that was contagious.

"Hi, Zoey!" His voice was overflowing with excitement. Or nervous energy. It was so endearing, in a boyish sort of way.

"Did you bring your credit card and a desire for some fun?" Zoey could've bitten her tongue off. What a rotten opening line to say to a guy who got snookered by a prostitute. But she didn't need to beat herself up. She was with a gentleman. And in being such, he only thought gentle things.

He nodded and with his hands still in his pocket said, "I'm ready. Did you want to grab a cab or should I call for a car?"

"Neither. I thought we would start at Barneys on Madison, try on some new clothes. It's about twenty blocks. It's a beautiful day. Let's stroll, if you don't mind."

"I'm game if you are."

They started walking. Zoey decided to hold off on the talk about how to stomp through the city with purpose. That speech would likely scare him right back into hiding. But there was something else. With Tristan next to her, she felt like taking her time. She wanted to enjoy all the smells and sounds, like the gyro and pretzels guys with their carts, music pumping out of storefronts, and people walking their dogs.

"Do you have ideas on what you want to do with me?" he asked.

"I was watching on the *Today* show this morning about the new spring fashions. Colors that are in and styles. Did you happen to see it?"

"Nope."

"What do you like to watch?"

"I don't have a TV. I like to read."

"And listen to music," she remined him with a knowing grin.

"That too." She couldn't be sure, but he may have started to blush.

When they reached the corner of Madison, they waited for the crossing light with a family, a mother who had a toddler by the hand and the dad pushing a stroller. They looked happy.

"Tell me about yourself?" Tristan asked. The timing was impeccable. Zoey stared at the baby carriage and debated just how much information she wanted to give him. "You said you were from Cleveland?"

"A suburb. I have one older sister, two younger sisters, and two younger brothers. My older sister, Ruth, is my roommate. Everyone else is still either at home or living near home."

"What made you want to move here?"

An innocent question. But also, a moment of truth.

"Adventure" was the answer she settled on. Not quite a lie, Zoey told herself. There was no need to drag him into her mess.

"Did you find it?"

"I certainly did. I'm having one right now," she quipped.

As they got closer to Barneys the crowds got thicker. People sidestepped one another in the effort to keep moving and retain their personal space. Others would abruptly stop and further mess up the flow of foot traffic. A man bumped into her with a disgusted "Geez." Zoey glanced at Tristan. His smile was gone, replaced with a grim expression, his hands still jammed in his pockets. Was he on the verge of a panic attack? She gingerly hooked her arm in his and began to match his step.

"He didn't even say 'excuse me,'" Tristan said.

"Hey. We're okay. We all have a right to the sidewalk. And I have pepper spray in my bag." She whispered up at him cheerfully in encouragement. "We only have a few more blocks to go."

He stared down at her, and she could feel him start to relax. She guided him over to the inside of the sidewalk, so that the faster walkers could hurry by.

"What do you like to read?"

"Everything! My favorite books are history. I have a library at home that's full of books. It's the one thing I had sent over from Paradise Cove. My grandfather devoured the military and war stuff. My grandmother loved her romances, so when you visit again and I show you the room, please don't judge. Although if I'm being honest, I have to admit, I've read almost all of them."

"If we're being honest, I guess I should admit . . . I've seen the room."

With their arms still hooked together he stopped short, looking down at her again, this time with a tilt of his head and laughter-filled eyes.

"What? You told me to make myself at home."

"You little devil," he said, and she wondered if he had picked up that come-hither look from those romance novels. He pulled her arm closer to his and they resumed their walking.

"I swear I didn't stay in any room long enough to take an inventory. I did notice you didn't have a television but thought maybe you had one hiding in a wall. And let me add, you are a heck of a housekeeper."

"Thank you." He continued to smile, unoffended by her confession. "Cleanliness is next to godliness, my grandmother used to say."

It was hard to believe they had known each other for only twenty-four hours. They had slipped into such easy conversation. Of course, Ruth had men who had proposed to her after one date, so it probably wasn't that big a deal. Zoey couldn't remember the last time she had let her guard down so quickly. They had reached their destination and unlocked arms, with Tristan opening the door and allowing her to enter the bustling building first. She led them straight to the men's department.

"Just so you know," Tristan said, "I do own a couple suits."

"I'm sure you do and I bet they're very nice. But I was thinking of us getting more in touch with your Steven Tyler side."

"I don't think I'm ready to start modeling leather pants yet." He was wary.

"How about a leather jacket?"

"Maybe."

Zoey shooed off the salesman asking if they needed help and went over to the folded jeans displays. She asked him his size and wrinkled her nose when he rattled off his thirty-two-inch waist, several inches smaller than her own. She stayed away from the ultraexpensive Saint Laurent and Balmain brands and began pulling jeans for him to try on, Rag & Bone, Citizens of Humanity, R13.

She dropped them in his waiting hands until the stack almost covered his face. He drew the line at ripped holes in the knees. The look on his face when she touched the ones that had been fake-rubbed with dirt or grass was laughable.

"I'm looking for stylish, not derelict," he stated firmly on his way to the dressing room. "My grandmother would roll over in her grave."

Zoey waited for him, sliding the shirt-holding hangers along the racks for colors that she thought would highlight his green eyes and bring out his all-around coloring.

"What do you think?" she heard from behind her.

She should have been ready for when she turned around. She knew from the leather pants episode that he had a hidden sexy. He had taken off his coat in the dressing room. Underneath it was a burnt orange velour V-neck long-sleeve shirt that he must've acquired back on the island. It was easily two sizes too small and clung to him like Saran wrap. Because the jeans were so low, it rode up to display a tiny portion of his flat belly, something he was able to avoid with the high-waisted pants he was used to. In short, he was magnificent.

He turned to give her a view from the back, and her jaw started to unhinge.

"Do they fit right?" Tristan said over his shoulder. "They feel so low, like they could fall off."

"They're skinny jeans," Zoey said, with her mouth suddenly dry. She wasn't sure about the old adage that "clothes make the man," but in this particular instance she would have to say clothes made this man hot as hell.

"I'm not skinny," he replied stubbornly. It was the first exhibition of him having any ego.

Zoey smiled and shook her head. "No, it's the style of jeans. Skinny jeans. Check the tag yourself if you don't believe me."

"Oh!" He tapped his forehead with three fingertips in a mock effort to turn on his brain. "Got it. I hope I don't have to bend over to pick anything up. They feel like they would take my underwear with them."

It took real effort to strive for casual and keep her eyes above his neck. "They look pretty good. They'll get softer. You'll get used to them. And we'll pick you out the right kind of belt."

Like leather. And long. Long enough to wrap around my wrists and then tie me to a bedpost, with those jeans slipping lower and lower as he does so, until he unzips them. . . .

Without realizing it, Zoey started biting down on her lower lip.

"What are you thinking about?" Tristan asked innocently.

"Um." Zoey turned her focus back to the racks to hide the telltale blush. "Shirts that will go with it. Why don't you go try on another pair?"

He came back out a few minutes later. "I think somebody already wore these and returned them."

She bit back a giggle. "Those are what is called the distressed look."

"Why? Because you feel dirty and uncomfortable wearing them?"

"No, silly. The denim is distressed. It's a process they put the material through to make them appear faded and worn. That's why it's mostly on the knees and thighs. Just think of it as the manufacturer breaking them in for you."

"If you say so. They are comfy though."

This time, Zoey was able to watch him walk back to the dressing room without fear of him catching her.

They spent the majority of the afternoon in Barneys. Tristan was the ultimate shopping companion. He didn't balk at any price tag and was willing to try on anything, even the garments he viewed skeptically, such as pants covered in studs or obvious bleach stains. And he was correct in his assessments: the more outrageous things didn't work for him.

"I don't mind distressed, as you call it. I just don't like sloppy," he told her, and Zoey agreed. Threadbare patches and strategically placed holes or tears were a little too much fashion for him to handle. Excessively baggy was a no-go as well, and Zoey was fine with that. He had hidden that spectacular physique long enough. Tristan fell in love with long shorts after telling her that all the shorts he owned fell above his knees.

"You mean like Bermuda shorts?" she asked.

"No," he replied seriously. "We got them right in St. Croix. But I don't know, maybe they were imported."

His adorable innocence was endless. In all, he ended up purchasing five pairs of jeans, three pairs of other pants that didn't settle under his armpits, six pairs of shorts, at least a dozen button-down shirts in various colors and patterns, and a slew of pullovers, polos, and sweaters. She picked out both brown and black leather belts but had no idea how to approach him about underwear, so she didn't. He even unwittingly indulged her fantasy by letting her pick out a leather jacket for him. They both agreed on a hooded bomber style after he complained about the other ones having too many zippers. Zoey didn't bother mentioning the other style made him look like a frightened Harley rider . . . or Fonzie. The jokes would likely have been wasted anyway. Zoey courteously stepped away and wandered the racks as he paid the exorbitant Barneys bill, telling him she'd meet him at the men's fragrance counter.

"How about an update to your cologne or aftershave?" Zoey asked when he met up with her, both his hands full of shopping bags.

Tristan grimaced. "I don't think so. I don't want to smell like a lady."

Zoey smiled to herself, thinking, *Baby steps.* She was able to talk him into a pomade though, for when he wanted a more updated look to his hair.

"It's time to ditch the part down the middle, dude," she suggested.

"Do you want to look for anything for yourself?" he asked, adding, "My treat, to thank you for all your help."

She could've told him a hundred things. Like friends don't have to reciprocate all the time, and just dressing him was all the treat she should be allowed for one day. Or that what he had paid her the night before was thanks enough. Or that she would rather be dragged behind a cross-town bus than have to model whatever she took into the dressing room, an exercise that would make her more distressed than the jeans he had to be talked into buying. She settled on, "Thanks, but I think I'm all shopped out."

"Then can I make you dinner? If you don't have any other plans, that is."

There was such a hopefulness to his voice. Luckily, she didn't have a job booked.

"That sounds awesome. I'd love to."

"Let's call my car service. These bags are weighing me down," he suggested.

"Sounds good to me."

"Can I borrow your phone? Or maybe Barneys will let me use theirs?"

"You forgot your phone?"

"I don't have one."

He had just spent so much money that someone from Barneys would've been willing to call them a car. Maybe even carry them both home on the salesman's back. Instead she handed Tristan her phone and thought, *This throwback-to-a-simpler-time stuff is getting ridiculous.*

Chapter 7

If Zoey lived to be a hundred, she doubted she would ever meet someone as courteous as Tristan. With him it wasn't an act or something he turned on and off. His grandparents had raised him well. He loaded the bags into the car himself and refused help from the doorman when they returned to his apartment.

Zoey sat on a stool at the island in the kitchen pondering her dilemma while he took his new clothes to his bedroom. When would she tell him about Derek? Should she just spit it out, or mention it in passing? Would he be disappointed in her? Would he put the instant kibosh on their friendship and ask her to leave? Things that others took for granted in this day and age were monumental to him. It wasn't like neglecting to tell him she got suspended from school for pot smoking or about having her tonsils taken out. She couldn't even say she was divorced. Whatever the outcome, she would have to face it then come to terms with it. The longer she waited, the worse it would be in the end. If he cooled off their friendship after hearing the news, it would sting. If they truly bonded, it would be heartbreaking, for both of them.

Music started playing from the overhead speakers. This time it was reggae. Just when Zoey thought she was on the verge of figuring him out, he threw her another surprise.

When Tristan returned, it was with a bottle of white wine and two long-stem wineglasses.

"How do you feel about Italian?" He opened a drawer and pulled out a corkscrew, driving the pointy end into the top of the bottle.

She watched him opening the liquid courage. "Always delicious. Tristan . . ."

The cork released with a resounding pop. He began to pour half glasses. "It's just a little glass of wine. I wanted to use it in the recipe tonight. It's too good to go to waste."

"Sounds wonderful." She was grateful for him presenting his back to put the bottle opener away. "Look, Tristan, there's something you should know. Not that I think it's a big deal, but I'm technically married."

She saw him stiffen again and he slowly closed the drawer before turning back to her. The expression on his face was new to her, tight-lipped anger.

"It's a very big deal. The word *technically* is just semantics. You're either married or you aren't."

The heat of his stare was enough to burn a hole right through her. "We're separated."

"Technically separated? Such as, I'm in Tristan's apartment and can't see my husband right now?"

If she wasn't feeling so awful about this latest misunderstanding, she would be able to appreciate the fire in his eyes. It was nice to know he wasn't a total pushover.

"My husband is back in Ohio and if I had my way, we would already be divorced. But I agreed to wait a year before filing. I thought it was ludicrous then and I think it still is now. But I agreed to it. I don't want to go back on my word."

She blinked back the tears that were burning her eyelids, furious that she couldn't stop the reaction or the shakiness in her voice.

"Did you run away from him because he abused you?"

His follow-up question was fraught with a different kind of anger, the chivalrous kind. The way all his muscles tensed in the too-small velour shirt, he looked perfectly capable of holding his own in a fight.

"He wasn't physically abusive," she said, forcing her gaze away from the sight of him. "But there's a lot of ways to abuse someone, you know?"

She stared at the white swirls in the black granite countertop until he slowly pushed her wineglass into her line of vision.

"It's going to be all right, Zoey," he said quietly. "I apologize for my initial overreaction. Thank you for being honest with me."

She looked back up into his eyes. All the kindness was back in them, and she was relieved. He had no interest in berating or casting judgment on her. "I'm never quite sure how to work it into conversation. 'Hi, my name is Zoey and I'm counting down the days till I can get a divorce' seems like overkill."

"Do you want to talk about it?" Tristan repeated the same question she had posed to him the night before. It was an open-ended invitation, not an interrogation.

She felt the lump in her throat starting to form. "There are so many ways my marriage went wrong, I don't know where to start."

He had gone back to puttering about the kitchen, pulling out pots and pans, going to the fridge to remove chicken, mushrooms, and eggs. He balanced all the items in his hands and plopped them down on the counter. Then he held up a stick of butter. He said very matter-of-factly, "I hope you're not one of those zealots who hates butter. Olive oil has its place too, but I prefer to use butter when I can."

"Do I look like I hate butter? Sometimes I use both. Everything's better with butter and batter."

Tristan picked up his wineglass and leaned against the counter. He extended it in a toast. "To new beginnings. All kinds."

Zoey picked up her glass as well, and from across the center island, they tapped them lightly together with a ping. "I think Derek was cheating on me. Plus he didn't fulfill one promise he made me before we married."

He quirked an eyebrow and chuckled. "I'm used to saying 'cheers,' but I guess that works too." Then he took a more serious tone. "I'm sorry that happened to you. I don't think a lot of people realize going in just how hard being married is."

"My parents made it look easy," she replied.

"My grandparents did too. They only talked about how hard it was."

Tristan was starting to assemble all the things he would need to make what Zoey guessed was Chicken Marsala. She felt so comfortable with him. The more they got to know each other, the more they seemed to have in common. He set up his work area the same way she did. And for the first time she was content to sit back and watch, instead of trying to jump in and actively participate. She wasn't sure how long being a spectator would last. He was still wearing the same clothes as when she picked him up that morning, despite now having a king's ransom's worth of new duds. She got the distinct impression that material things didn't really matter to him; people did. It likely made his self-imposed solitude all the more frustrating, even if he didn't show it. He was a fascinating specimen.

"Derek kept saying he wants to start a family." Zoey said the words for the first time out loud. Ruth was the only one who knew about Derek's pressure of trying to get her to conceive.

Tristan turned around from the counter. "And you don't?"

She toyed with the stem of her wineglass. "Even when I believed our marriage was on solid ground, every time someone asked me when I'm going to have a baby, I wanted to scream. Does that make me a horrible person?"

"Certainly not. It's your body, you call the shots."

In one sentence, the man who knew her just over twenty-four hours was able to break it down to its most basic principle. He got it.

"I have nothing against kids, but I had four younger siblings," she continued to explain, because she wanted to, not because she felt she had to justify. "Not that my parents were lying down on the job, but Ruth and I were expected to help out. Ruth was . . . is . . . the fun one. I'm the conscientious one, the worrier, the perfectionist. Ruth fought for her right to party, which gave me one more person to worry about and have to take care of. I put in my time changing diapers and warming bottles and chasing after toddlers."

He was studying her, listening to her, periodically nodding in agreement but saying nothing.

"And I know that no matter what he says, deep down inside he only wants to start a family to keep me under his thumb. So he can be free to go and do what he likes while I'm stuck at home being responsible for the life we created. He never talked about wanting children while we were dating."

Tristan finally spoke. "He wants to take advantage of all your best qualities. That's not right."

"To be fair, I'm not much better than he is. We'd been together on and off since eighth grade. He played sports, was popular, didn't go to college because he thought he already knew everything there was to know. I bought into all of that. Derek had a real take-on-the-world attitude. But it was all puffing. He's lazy and always looking for the easiest way to do things instead of the right way. I never in my wildest dreams thought I was settling for someone who peaked in high school. I wanted to move away and try new things, but he was content to stay right where he was. By the time I figured it out, it was too late."

"That's what I like about you, Zoey. You're not only a thinker, you're also willing to take some responsibility for your situation. And take it from one who knows, it's never too late to make a change."

He went back to making dinner and she went back to sipping her wine.

"For what it's worth, babies seem like a lot of hard work. They're not toys, they're people. And this world is a dangerous place. If you can't commit, you shouldn't."

They were silent for a spell, lost in their own thoughts. But it wasn't long before Tristan shifted his eyes up from what he was doing with a small knowing grin.

"You're just dying to do something, aren't you?"

She smiled back with a little roll of her eyes. "This is the sort of kitchen that inspires cheffery."

"Chef-fer-y? That's a new one."

"I made it up," Zoey said brightly, getting up off her barstool to join him. He tossed her an onion and she pulled out a knife from the drawer where she knew he kept them. He handed her a small plastic cutting board. They were back to working in unison and the mood became lighter. It wasn't long before Zoey was jammin' to the music.

"This music is awesome," she commented, stepping away from her task to fight back onion tears. He picked up a mallet with spikes on one side.

"I discovered the radio station that played it in St. Croix," he said, banging on the chicken breasts to flatten them. "It was during my teenage rebel years. My grandparents knew eventually I would get sick of listening to all their Perry Como and Frank Sinatra records. Still, they checked my eyes for months to see if I was smoking 'the funny stuff.'"

"Were you?"

Zoey was nearly floored when he gave a careless shrug and replied, "A couple of times."

She stepped away from the onion again, this time to stare at him, aghast.

"Don't look at me that way," he protested. "The island is full of it. They did fire the landscaper once they found out he was the one I was smoking it with."

"I used to love smoking pot," Zoey said wistfully.

"Did you want me to try and get you some?" Tristan asked, clearly disappointed in her statement. "Those pharmaceutical people from last night told me they could get me almost anything. Come to think of it, so did one of the overnight doormen when I first moved in."

"Oh no." Zoey was quick with her reply, although she would've given her eyeteeth to see what he would be like after a bong hit or two. "I should clarify. I wanted to be a pot smoker but I was never able to make an exact connection. I would watch movies and TV shows where people made one call and it was delivered right to their door. I was always having to go through like two or three people to score any. It got to be a hassle. It felt like begging. I took it as a sign that it wasn't supposed to be my vice, so I just got over it."

"I like you much better virtuous," he said with relief.

"Don't get carried away."

Together they playfully finished making dinner. Zoey minced cloves of fresh garlic and tossed some into the spinach Tristan was sautéing. She filled a large pot with water and went to search the pantry for some penne she remembered seeing. He was going back to the fridge for some fresh mozzarella and they banged into each other. For Zoey, it was like smacking into a wall. So much unexpected muscle to come up against, she nearly bounced off him.

"Whoa there," he said after the contact, grabbing her by the shoulders to steady her. His grip was firm, his hands large. Nobody had touched her in almost a year, and her response was like a jolt of electricity coursing through her. She could smell his sweet wine-tinged breath and fought off a head rush.

"Sorry." She ducked her head so he wouldn't see her visceral reaction. After that, it was Zoey's turn to make sure there was adequate space between them.

Tristan had created a most delicious dish. After lightly frying the chicken, he topped it with the spinach and cheese and put it in the oven with a mushroom and white wine sauce to finish up. They carried their plates and what remained of the wine into the dining room. Then they both ate like they were going to the electric chair, devouring every morsel.

"I'm glad we decided against a salad or bread," Zoey said after the last bite was consumed and she was wiping her mouth with a cloth napkin, feeling not an ounce of regret for her part in polishing off her half of a box of pasta. "This dish was amazing."

"Just my version of cheffery," he quipped, reaching for his wineglass. Afterward, he offered to move the party to the library to have dessert.

"Forget dessert. I have no room left," she said with a satisfied sigh, wishing she could unbutton her jeans. "And I'd much rather see some of the art."

"Do you want to start with impressionist, mosaic,

or modern?" he asked excitedly, rising to pull out her chair for her.

"Let's go with impressionists," she said.

"Do you know art?"

"Don't have a clue."

Tristan laughed and grabbed both their wineglasses before leading her down the hall. "Then I guess I don't need to worry about you telling the reals from the fakes. Allow me to enlighten you a bit. Impressionism started in the nineteenth century. You can tell it mainly by all the small, thin brushstrokes, usually oil paints. Mosaics are pieces made up of small stones, pieces of glass, or tiles. Basically, materials that are flat, small, square, and colorful. The impressionist style is named after Claude Monet's work *Impression, soleil levant*, the translation meaning *Impression, Sunrise*."

"I've heard of him!" she exclaimed, mainly from having seen the movie *Titanic* over a dozen times. As they entered the room, she brought her voice down to a whisper. The lights turned on automatically, bathing the room in a soft glow with single-bulb lights that shone directly on the artworks themselves. "Do you have one of them? You know, the *Sunrise* one?"

"It just so happens that I do." Tristan handed over her wineglass and sat down on the long leather bench in the center of the room, patting the space beside him. "Come. We're right in front of it."

"Is yours real?" she whispered, sitting down next to him.

"No." He gave her an indulgent smile. "The real *Sunrise* is in Paris."

"Oh." She giggled at her own ignorance. "Sorry."

"Don't be," he teased. "It's probably happy there."

They sat in silence, sipping their wine and looking at the serene picture, with all its mostly pale tones of the sky and sea, with the exception of the bright orange spot that made up the sun and the strokes of orange that served as its reflection on the water.

Zoey could understand why he found the rooms of art so inviting. The speakers here were turned down to enhance the ambiance. It was peaceful and quiet, with only the faint sounds of music thumping in the distance. She could hear him breathing. It was profoundly romantic.

Hold up. Not that word. Not here. Not with this guy.

"It's getting late," she said, breaking the silence that just a moment ago was comfortable and now was charged with an energy she had no business experiencing. She stood up. "I should probably go."

She didn't know if he felt it too, but he didn't try to make her stay. He rose as well. "Can I call you a car? Walk you home?"

"No thanks." She gave him a smile but refrained from looking him in the eye. "I'm going to race-walk off the penne."

She couldn't get out of his apartment fast enough. She needed fresh air on her face. She needed to clear her head from the long-dormant feelings that suddenly threatened to surface. Whether that was from the wine or the company, now was not the time to analyze it. He helped her into her jacket and she gathered her purse, all the while thinking about how if the circumstances were different, she'd be wanting and waiting for a good-night kiss. A kiss she would've been willing to initiate. A kiss that she could only imagine would be as thorough and thought out as all the other things he did. It only added to her fluster.

"Are you busy tomorrow?" Tristan asked, opening the door.

"I am," she replied, eternally grateful she didn't have to lie to him. She would need at least a day to get herself back in check. "I'm catering a brunch in Tribeca for a very nice lady and her new in-laws. It should be interesting."

"Good luck with that. Not that you need it."

She got out to the street and took a gulp of air. She began walking briskly in the direction of home, lecturing herself the entire way. With his initial reaction to the news she was married, it wasn't hard to surmise that even if he felt a fraction of the chemistry she just did, he wouldn't act on it. She needed to build his confidence and get him up to speed to meet the woman of his dreams. She couldn't fail him as a friend or violate his trust.

But she was ashamed of herself for just how many ways she wanted to.

Chapter 8

Tristan communicated with Zoey every day, with the first time being an unexpected text. Zoey was home after the in-law brunch, feeling the rush that came with success. Her eggs Benedict were perfection. The poached whites of the eggs were fully cooked, and the yolks showed no signs of hardening. The hollandaise sauce just the right consistency. The potatoes that accompanied them were crunchy on the outside and soft inside with just the right amounts of peppers and onions to make them savory. She squeezed her own orange juice for the mimosas. All the fruit in her fruit salad was ripe and delectable. She went above and beyond to make sure her stressed-out host looked like the lady of the manor in her mother-in-law's eyes.

She walked away with a one-hundred-dollar tip for her efforts.

She was in the middle of a postwork nap when her phone pinged. She almost didn't answer it, fearing that it was Derek, who had already sent several texts since she hung up on him two days prior. With one eye closed, she picked up the phone to confirm and saw an unknown number and the words: HELLO OUT THERE!

Curious, she wrote back: HI. I THINK YOU HAVE THE WRONG NUMBER.

After less than a minute she got: ZOEY?

She had a sneaking suspicion, which made her smile, but asked anyway: WHO IS THIS?

IT'S TRISTAN. I WENT OUT AND GOT A PHONE TODAY. ALL BY MYSELF.

LOL

YOU THINK YOU'RE TRICKY, BUT I KNOW WHAT THAT MEANS.

OH YEAH? WHAT DOES IT MEAN?

LEFT OVER LAUGHTER

CLOSE. IT MEANS LAUGH OUT LOUD

I KNEW THAT, SO LOL ON YOU. WHY ARE YOU LAUGHING AT ME?

I WASN'T REALLY. IT'S ONE OF THOSE THINGS YOU
WRITE WHEN SOMEONE SAYS SOMETHING FUNNY.
OR YOU DON'T HAVE A READY RESPONSE.

WHICH ONE IS IT FOR YOU?

A LITTLE OF BOTH. MOSTLY YOUR ALL BY YOURSELF
COMMENT. PROUD OF YOU.

**ONE OF MY NEW JACKETS HAS AN INSIDE POCKET
SPECIFICALLY FOR A PHONE, SO I THOUGHT IT
WAS TIME.**

He texted her every day. Usually nothing more than
a hello, or wishing her a nice day. Sometimes she would
start a conversation. Other times she would thank him
and wish him the same. But she made sure to text
him something worth learning daily. It was usually an
often-used acronym, though he was too proper and set
in his ways to use them, preferring to spell out each
word in its entirety.

With the distance, Zoey was able to regain some
of her equilibrium. Tristan was out of sight, but not
quite out of mind. She suffered through Ruth's un-
invited half-hour diatribe about how men and women
are incapable of being just friends. It was all the more
disconcerting because Zoey had made no mention to
her sister about the way she fled his apartment when
her thoughts turned to departing the friend zone. But

Zoey had to be careful. Getting too defensive would only give Ruth more ammunition.

"That's ridiculous," Zoey argued.

"No matter what anybody says, one side or the other is in it for the attraction." Ruth did everything short of pointing her finger at Zoey in accusation.

"What about gay people?"

"That's a nonissue. A gay man being friends with a woman is different because there's no chance of sex. The same applies to gay women being friends with straight men."

"Okay, so then by your theory all the lesbians you're friends with are really wanting to hit on you?"

That stumped Ruth enough to make her drop the argument. But it also gave Zoey a lot of food for thought. In the end, Zoey laid the blame on the wine for her reaction to Tristan.

That didn't stop Zoey from feeling a mixture of panic and thrill when Tristan texted her early Friday morning.

I THINK I'M READY TO GO OUT AND EXPERIENCE THE NIGHTLIFE. WOULD YOU LIKE TO JOIN ME?

Zoey doubted he would follow through if she declined. Or maybe not. He was known for jumping right into the deep end. Maybe it was time to get him out there. The sooner he embraced all New York City had to offer, the sooner she would be able to get back to her own agenda. The clock was ticking, and she wanted to make sure she had enough to afford a lawyer if Derek tried to fight simple mediation. Besides, it was common knowledge that once somebody found a significant other, all their other playmates were slowly left in the dust. What's the worst that could happen, he would begin to develop a network of friends?

"Okay, Ruth, now's your chance." Zoey looked up from her phone after responding to Tristan that it sounded like a great idea. "Tristan wants to go out and party. Not only can you meet him, but I can also prove to you that my motives are pure and his are innocent."

Ruth immediately started making plans for Saturday night.

Saturday afternoon Zoey took her first long look in the mirror. She'd just survived another hectic kid's birthday party. It was easy money menu-wise, but murder having to listen to a bunch of kids screaming up and down the stairs of a Brooklyn brownstone all while keeping a smile plastered on her face. After a much-needed shower, Zoey gave her reflection a long-overdue assessment and was not thrilled with the final analysis. She always wore the same clothes for working, black pants and a white shirt. Her hair was always tied back for sanitary reasons. She avoided makeup—it was a total waste once she started sweating over the stove. When she wasn't working, it was jeans or yoga pants and whatever shirt she put a hand on first. She stared at herself in the mirror. She had the nerve to think Tristan needed a makeover? Well, charity begins at home. With a heavy sigh, she began opening vanity drawers and shuffling stuff around, not sure what she was looking for.

At the back of one drawer, she spied teeth-whitening strips. It was as good a place to start as any. Who doesn't appreciate a bright white smile? Zoey read the instructions on the box and pulled out a package for both her upper and lower teeth. They seemed so large, even after folding them in and anchoring them to the back of her teeth. They had a slimy feel and a faint aftertaste. She double-checked the package. She needed to wear them for thirty minutes. Sigh. She checked her phone for the time and left the bathroom. She turned on the television and sat down on her futon to wait. Clamping her jaw shut was increasing the slight pounding at her temple. Before long, she was leaning her head back against the futon. The next thing she knew, Ruth was gently shaking her awake.

"Hey," Ruth said. "What time do you have to meet Mr. Manners?"

"What time is it now?" was Zoey's still-drowsy and mumbled response. Her mouth was dry as a bone, and her lips felt chapped.

"Almost five thirty."

"FIVE THIRTY?!?" Zoey jumped up and made a run for the bathroom, stubbing her toe on the coffee table in the process. She hopped down the hall, making random grabs at her pulsating foot with one hand and ripping the film out of her mouth with the other. There was no time to check for blood or broken bones. She'd kept the teeth-whitening strips in her mouth for nearly four hours.

She didn't need to turn on the light in the bathroom to get a good look, but Zoey did it anyway. With her mouth still tightly shut, she stood in front of the mirror and took a deep breath. She gave her reflection a shaky smile.

Zoey had often thought she showed too much of her gums when she smiled. That problem had been solved. Zoey's teeth didn't look all that much different. Her gums, however, were bleached completely white. From where her teeth met the gum line all the way to where it attached to her lips. It was impossible to tell where her teeth ended and her gums began, making her mouth look like it was all teeth. Even her tongue had spots of discoloration.

Zoey took big handfuls of water and repeatedly rinsed her mouth out. It lessened the icky taste in her mouth but did nothing to weaken the brightness of all that white. She tried to brush her teeth, but the mistreated gums were sensitive, and she was afraid they would bleed. She was already envisioning the gums sloughing off and leaving her with nothing but exposed bone.

She tried to talk herself down. It was going to be dark. She would adjust her smile a bit. She tried a few subdued, controlled grins in the mirror. The ones that didn't look faked and pained resembled lecherous grins. Maybe every time someone said something witty, she could put her glass up to her mouth and take a drink. Suddenly heavy drinking sounded like a good idea.

"You okay in there?" Ruth gave a quick knock.

"Fine," Zoey sang. After all the arguing, the last thing she needed was her sister suspecting she was going to any special lengths for going out tonight. It was bad enough she suspected Zoey was harboring secret feelings for Tristan. She closed her mouth and opened the door.

"You took off like a bat out of hell there." Ruth leaned against the doorway and crossed her arms. "Is your toe all right?"

"Yeah." Zoey gave a quick glance to the slight bruise that was starting to form at the tip of her pinky toe. She put the toilet lid down, set the foot with the injured toe on top of it, and bent down to examine it, moving it around so she'd appear to be checking if it was broken. It was the perfect excuse to keep her sister from getting a look into her mouth. "I guess no dancing for me tonight. I told Tristan I would meet him at his place around seven."

But Ruth wasn't paying Zoey much mind. In fact, it looked like she had stopped listening. Her attention was focused on the box of tooth-whitening strips that Zoey had left on the counter. She was studying it, with a perplexed look on her face. Then Ruth shrugged and plucked the box off the counter, then tossed it in the trash.

"I meant to throw these out. There is something wrong with them. They didn't do a damn thing for my teeth."

Zoey didn't know whether she wanted to laugh, cry, or scream but she refrained from making a choice because all of them would involve opening her mouth.

Chapter 9

Zoey decided to wear one of the two dresses she'd brought with her when she fled Ohio. It was nothing like Ruth's cocktail dress, black, form fitting, thigh high, and complete with the dreaded bared arms and matching four-inch heels. Zoey's was a more reserved royal blue with three-quarter sleeves and a flared skirt that fell just above her knees. She accessorized with black tights, ballet flats, and a half sweater jacket. She had much bigger things to worry about, namely her blinding white gums. Zoey blow-dried her hair and left it down, applied a little blush, shadow, mascara, and lip gloss, then made for the door. Not wanting to break a sweat from either exertion or anxiety, she left, telling Ruth they would meet up with her at the bar, and skipped the walking, taking a cab uptown. The entire ride she practiced ways she could be sparkly and talkative without having to fully open her mouth.

She forgot about her dilemma entirely when Tristan answered the door upon her arrival. It's easy to keep your teeth covered when your mouth drops open.

He was wearing his skinny jeans, with a button-down white-and-black-striped shirt and a gray two-button slim-fit jacket with lapels. A jacket she didn't remember from their trip to Barneys. He must have taken the initiative and ventured out on his own. He had used the pomade, but she still detected the scent of Old Spice, so he hadn't gone hog wild. Ruth was going to lose her mind when she got a gander, and that was problematic, for a multitude of reasons.

"Wow." Zoey nodded approvingly. "You do clean up nice."

"Lady, you are on fleet!" Tristan said in appreciation, stepping back for her to enter.

"Thank you. I think."

"Maybe that's not it." He shook his head before trying again. "You are on FREAK!"

"I'm not sure what you're trying to tell me."

"That you look perfect," he replied before pausing, then saying softly, "Beautiful. In every way."

He was so open. Honest. It was so refreshing not to have to fend off all the machismo, the posturing.

Zoey resisted the urge to wrap her arms around his neck and go in with both lips. Although *on fleet* may have applied last Memorial Day weekend, she mused, when Ruth had more sailors floating through their apartment than the USS *Independence.* "I think the word you are looking for is *fleek.* You are on fleek."

And he was.

"On fleek?" Tristan repeated, adding a chuckle. "I think I'm going to have to start paying more attention. But either way, you are it."

Zoey felt her cheeks start to heat up under his gaze. "Thanks. And don't worry, you shouldn't be talking like that anyway, unless you just graduated from high school."

When she got to the living room, another surprise was waiting for her. Mounted above the fireplace was a seventy-inch television. To her horror, it was on the E! channel, where the programming was almost exclusively about the rich, beautiful, and famous.

"I see you got a new toy."

"I did. Did you know this thing has over three hundred channels? Mind boggling."

"Have you christened it with an extensive channel surf?"

"I'm ashamed to say it's been on for days and I can't tear myself away."

"Watch anything good?" she said, covertly trying to see how much damage control was going to be needed.

He scrunched up his face in thought. "Hmmm. Well, apparently housewives exist all over the country and they spend all their time together, even though it's clear they despise each other. There are people who weigh over six hundred pounds and I guess there is only one doctor in Texas that wants to help them, and he does it by removing part of their stomachs. I found out there are people who are called hoarders that have so much nasty stuff in their homes they can't move around. I like how people come to the rescue and help them, but I'm still worried for them. Oh, and there's a crazy lady who owns a dance school for young girls who spends most of her time being mean to them and screaming. And the mothers tolerate it!"

"Look, those are called reality shows, but there is nothing real about them. Those shows are mostly staged. They have directors and producers and make sure that no matter how much film footage they take of the people, they only broadcast the parts that are outrageous. Do yourself a favor and stick to game shows or comedies."

"There was one other thing I noticed. People on this channel right here? They go to see plastic surgeons a lot. Don't like your face? Change it. Breasts or backside too big or too small, go under the knife and wake up with your heart's desire. Apparently, there is no ugly, there's only poor. Tragic really, since most of them look just fine. Nobody seems as concerned with being a good person."

He sounded sad. Zoey wondered if she had done the right thing, trying to break him out of his media blackout. It was starting to feel like she was the one in need of a makeover.

"That's enough of that," Tristan said, grabbing the remote on the mantel and turning the television off, bringing them both back to the moment.

"What do you feel like having for dinner? There are some great restaurants in Chelsea near where Ruth is meeting us later. We have plenty of time." Zoey rolled her eyes. "The club doesn't open till eleven."

Tristan's reaction was nothing short of glee. "We may stay out all night! Very exciting."

Zoey smiled at his delight. She just couldn't help it. His enthusiasm was infectious.

Tristan's smile instantly faded. "Do you feel all right?"

She gave him a bemused look and then remembered. "I'm fine. I fell asleep with these strips that make your teeth whiter in my mouth. I ended up bleaching my gums."

He didn't laugh. "Your teeth are already white. And you can barely notice it. I'm just captivated by your smile. It lit up my whole apartment the first time I met you."

Zoey had heard about how happy people only see the good in others, and Tristan was living proof. Then she smelled it, dumbfounded that she hadn't noticed before. The faint smell of onions and garlic and . . . was that thyme? She actually lifted her nose in the air to see if she could decipher any other spices.

"I can see you answered your own question about dinner this evening," Tristan said with a grin. "I haven't completely lost my roots. Tonight, I want to show off some of the first things I learned to cook from the islands."

They went into the dining room, and it almost took her breath away. The table once again was beautifully set. The floral arrangement was new, a huge glorious bouquet, not of romantic roses, but tulips and sunflowers, purple asters and daisies. It was placed directly in between and above the two place settings at one end of the table. In another life, she might have swooned.

"Sit," he said, pulling out her chair. "It's all ready and in the warming tray."

He dashed off, returning with two bowls and setting one in front of her then taking his own seat.

"This is callaloo soup, although I used spinach. I got the idea a little too spur of the moment and had spinach left over from the other day." Tristan stopped when she raised an eyebrow. "Yes, I used week-old spinach, but it's a soup, for crying out loud."

"Didn't seem to affect it," Zoey said after taking a spoonful. "This is delicious."

He brought out the main course and Zoey was blown away. "This is unreal!"

Tristan grinned with pride. "This is Fish and Okra Fungi. Normally, you would cook the fish in a saucepan, but I broiled it. The fish is fresh, but I didn't want to run the risk of stinking up my kitchen. And I love the smell of the cornmeal cooking, so, yeah, I'm selfish like that."

Then he took his napkin and tucked it into his shirt at the neck like a bib. Zoey laughed behind her napkin.

"If I drop something on these clothes, I'll kill myself. It took me all day to pick out this outfit."

He was onto something there. Zoey tucked her napkin into the neckline of her dress as well.

The fungi wasn't as spicy as Zoey thought it would be, but there was plenty of pepper and onion. The cornmeal had a marvelous texture, and Tristan proved his love of butter. Instead of her original plan to only pick at her food to keep from bloating, Zoey once again was cleaning her plate while their easy conversation flowed.

"Do you miss home?" Zoey asked.

"I used to." Tristan smiled at her from across the table. "I wanted to make a change, but I had no idea just how big a change New York was. Or just how well my grandparents had sheltered me. Lately, I don't miss it so much. I have you to thank for that."

"Wasn't there anyone else you trusted to show you the ropes?"

Tristan paused, put down his fork, and stared at her hard. It felt like he was looking through her, trying to see inside her. He placed his elbows on the table and made a steeple with pointer fingers over his mouth. It looked like he was praying for a sign on whether or not he should confess something.

"I've seen things, Zoey. I've seen things and I know things."

The words and the way he said them were gloomy, with a touch of chilling.

"The key to my success was also to my paranoia, I'm afraid," he continued. "It was all right in front of my face and I missed it. Once I made the discovery and realized I should've known better, I started to question my own ability. About everything."

"I'm trying to follow, but I don't get it." Zoey set down her fork. "Is this about your work?"

He paused again, then nodded. "It is. Sort of."

No help there. "Tristan, I don't want you to betray a confidence, but if you're worried about whether or not you can trust me, I promise you that you can."

"It's not so much about trust. It's more about not wanting to stick you in the same boat with me."

"I'm smart. And I'm strong. Try me."

He took a moment to measure his words. "The software I created enables the government to learn as much as they want to about its citizens with the touch of a button. Do you realize the implications of that? They can know where you are at any given time. Who you know. What you like and don't like. What scares you. I'm not saying that they use it for nefarious purposes, but it only takes one bad apple to make another person's life a living hell. The thought of that crushes me."

"If it wasn't you inventing the program, it would've been someone else."

"Still, it's an invasion of privacy. Even more frightening is the number of people who found out and have approached me to create something similar for them. I became the go-to guy without saying a word. I decided to hide in plain sight, stay away from social media and the online world. I only use my computer to order my clothes and my groceries." Tristan gave her a little wink. "Or at least I used to."

"Sounds like your world got awfully big really fast. That's enough to overwhelm anyone. And paranoia is like an open wound—if you don't do something to treat it, it's bound to fester. I let my mind run away with me too, sometimes, but the solution is to go out into the world and live your life. The way you want to live it. In another ten years, everyone will know everything about another person with the touch of a button anyway."

Tristan threw back his head and laughed. "I knew you would understand. The more time I spend with you, the more I realize I—what's the phrase—can't fight city hall? And I don't think I want to anymore. At least not tonight."

"Speaking of tonight, what are your goals, Tristan?" Zoey knew she didn't have to ask him about the random hookup scenario or getting blitzed off his rocker, but she also wanted to be sure exactly what her role was supposed to be.

"I don't know," he responded, some of his shyness returning. He got up to clear the plates and she picked up her own before he could stop her. Together they took them back to the kitchen. "Maybe meet someone who wants to dance?"

Chapter 10

I could really get used to this, Zoey thought on the quiet ride back across town in the back of a cushy Mercedes.

There were so many amazing things about New York City, and one of them was how alive it became the later it got. Back in Ohio, the sidewalks were empty well before midnight. The "nightclub" that Derek worked in was little more than a bar with a dance floor and a house DJ on Saturday nights. It closed at 1:00 A.M. and the parking lot was a ghost town by two. In Manhattan, the streets were just beginning to buzz with nightlife at midnight, especially on Saturday nights. Zoey wondered if it would have been better to start with something less manic, like a Broadway show?

She should have known by now that Tristan Malloy was full of surprises.

Their destination was a nightclub called Marquee, on Tenth Avenue. It was a hot spot that Zoey was familiar with only from Ruth's frequent chatter. It was a place that Zoey feared Ruth had chosen not for Tristan's comfort, but to show off. When the car pulled up in front of the building, the line outside was already long. The bouncers standing guard at the door were looking straight ahead. Clearly nobody would be flirting their way in tonight. Zoey hoped all of Ruth's bragging was not her sister just blowing smoke or they'd be looking for another venue ASAP.

"You ready?" she asked Tristan as he reached for her hand to help her out of the car.

"Let's do this thing," he replied.

"Before we head to the back of the line, let me call my sister. She's probably already in there." Zoey pulled out her phone from her tiny handbag, then heard her name being called.

"Zoe!"

They turned around to find Ruth and her girlfriends, in fabulous faux furs and stiletto heels. They were standing in the middle of the line with the rest of the crowd. Great.

Ruth was clearly miffed, which seemed appropriate, because so was Zoey.

"What is this?" Zoey asked as she approached the

velvet rope that separated them, careful not to appear like she was going to cut in line, not that it mattered. The line wasn't moving, and the only activity was from people walking past them with the smug looks of VIPs. It looked like everyone standing outside was going to be waiting a long time. "I thought you had an in here?"

"There's some big party going on," Ruth told her defensively, her fingers tapping wildly on her phone.

"I tried calling for tickets when we got here, and they were all sold out," Ruth's friend Abbie chimed in. Her voice would best be described as half excuse, half complaint.

"Who is she texting with?" Zoey jerked a thumb in her sister's direction.

"Blake. He's part of the bachelor party going on in there, taking up all the space."

"I only chose this place because he said it would be fun," Ruth grumbled at her screen. "Sure, fun for him, he got in."

Blake Burton was an attorney in the legal department where Ruth and the girls worked. Recently divorced and in his early thirties, he was determined to get back into the swing and had spent the last six months saying yes to any sort of group activity. It started with lunch, and soon he was invited every weekend to join in whatever they were doing. Sometimes he brought friends, but he was no dummy—why share the company of the four or more girls? He also came in handy when one of the ladies needed to brush off unwanted attention in a hurry—he was always happy to pose as someone's boyfriend.

"This may be a blessing in disguise," Zoey said with a returning optimism as she looked down the never-ending line of increasingly anxious partyers. This place might be a little much for Tristan on his first clubbing adventure. "Why don't we take the party someplace a little more—"

"Zoey!" She heard her name being called. When she turned toward the direction of the sound, she found Tristan not only standing near the front door, but also waving them over.

Zoey and Tristan waited at the door while Ruth and her friends weaved their way through the mass of people on their side of the velvet rope.

"What did you just do here?" It was a question that didn't need asking, but she wanted the verification. The mere fact that he was able to engage the stoic door-men in dialogue could only mean one thing.

He gave her a sly grin. "Money talks."

"How much exactly did you slip these guys?"

"Now that's just impolite," he told her with a newly confident and adorable wink. Then he turned his attention to Ruth and her friends, who had caught up. "Good evening, ladies. I'm Tristan."

Zoey watched with mounting irritation as Ruth and the girls openly looked Tristan up and down and greeted him with coy smiles.

Not only were they let into the club, but someone was waiting to lead them over to a single booth on the first floor, right near the bar but not below the DJ setup or too close to the dance floor. It was a prime location in a club that was rapidly becoming packed to the rafters.

"I call bullshit." Ruth got up close to Zoey's ear to be heard above the noise as she walked closely behind her after they checked their coats, except for Tristan, who didn't want to break up his ensemble. "This dude is way too smooth."

While Zoey would've liked nothing better than to scream back in Ruth's face, she settled for a careless backward wave of her hand and a shake of her head as she kept one eye on Tristan's back and the other on the people who were mingling and dancing. The whole bar was thumping with the LED lighting flashing to the music. She was no longer worried about Tristan having a panic attack as much as she was about all of them having epileptic seizures. Now she knew why her sister often never heard a word Zoey said to her the day after clubbing.

Waiting at the table was a server, with a bottle of Dom Pérignon chilling in a bucket next to the table. Zoey watched Tristan move in close to the ear of the server, who bobbed her head repeatedly as her smile grew wider. Then she popped the cork on the bottle and filled the glasses before leaving. Tristan placed a glass in each of the girls' hands before raising his own in a wordless toast. Above the din, Zoey could hear them all shout "Cheers!" except for Abbie, who said "*L'chaim!*" and Erin, who shouted "*Salud!*"

Then Ruth ordered them all shots of Belvedere and, with the help of her friends, pulled Tristan to the dance floor, leaving Zoey behind to fume at the table alone.

She craned her neck to watch them all form a tight circle around Tristan, shaking their booties to the pulsing beat that reverberated against her eardrums. From the glimpses that she was able to catch of him, he looked like he was having the time of his life, completely in his element, not like someone who was trying something for the first time. Simmer was ratcheted up to seething. But she had no vested interest in him, Zoey reminded herself. And jealousy had never been her bag.

The server dropped off the shots and Zoey's gaze traveled over the five tiny glasses lined up in front of her and she briefly deliberated whether drinking them all would make her feel better or worse.

To his credit, Tristan was still too reserved to cut loose the way she had seen him do in the privacy of his own home. But he was able to find the bass line with ease, and Zoey's eyes became glued to him.

"Didn't anyone ever tell you that pretty girls aren't supposed to drink alone?"

Zoey looked up at the faint sound of the voice. It was a man, and a handsome one at that. And young, possibly a year or two out of college. He was sporting one of those expensive tattered sweaters. He also had a close-cut beard that outlined his jaw, and a small mustache to match.

He took a seat without being invited, forcing Zoey to slide over to accommodate him. And she did, thinking, *Why not?* It was better than being the matron table monitor.

"I'm not alone. I'm on roofie patrol, watching the drinks," she said, pushing one of the shots in front of him. "Go ahead and make my job easier."

"Join me!"

All the yelling to be heard over the music was giving her a headache. She held up her champagne glass to appease him. She watched him down the shot and give the little head shake that often accompanies the action. The music had switched up and she watched as the rest of her party started returning to the table. She felt a surge of satisfaction when she saw Tristan's smile become tight and guarded as he made his approach.

"Everything okay here, Zoey?" She lip-read him perfectly.

She gave a bright smile and said, "It's fine," not caring if he could hear her. Ruth's friends were already squeezing in beside him and yelling their introductions, with Ruth leaning over the table to make hers, treating college boy to a healthy shot of cleavage. Zoey slid over to the far end of the booth, grateful that this was one of those problems that was going to take care of itself.

Tristan sat down next to her before she could leave the booth entirely. The girls tried to hand him his shot, but he waved it off with a point to the other man, who happily drank that one as well. The music switched again, had slowed down. For the first time since they arrived Zoey didn't have to scream her own thoughts to hear herself think. Then she felt a faint brush of fingertips down her forearm. The kind of touch that set her skin to tingle.

"Dance with me," he said as he stood back up and held out his hand. It was the first time he hadn't asked for her permission on something. It was more of a gentle command. She took it and let him lead her to the dance floor. The last time Zoey had done any dancing was at her wedding. She didn't care. He found them some space, gave her a twirl, and when he stopped, they were face-to-face.

And they danced. They began to move with the music. Zoey was clumsy at first, feeling like she was dancing in cement shoes. She closed her eyes to try and block everything out and find the rhythm. When she found the beat and reopened them, his stare was still fixed on her, intense and overwhelming. She looked down at her feet.

Tristan moved in close for a moment to bring his mouth to her ear. "Relax, girlfriend, we're doing fine."

Zoey looked back up and this time was able to recognize the elation in his eyes. It was like he had given her an engraved invitation to cut loose. She accepted.

They swayed and grooved in unison, their gazes now locked on each other. They didn't touch, didn't bump or grind. But it was sensual, oh, so sensual, and Zoey felt all the other dancers fade off into the background until it was the two of them alone on the dance floor. His arms didn't freakishly flail. His feet didn't look like he was stomping grapes. All the energy and motion generated from his hips. Music was putting him at ease, and Zoey was eager to follow him there. It ended much too soon. When the song was over and the spell was broken, he extended an arm for her to walk ahead of him back to the table, and she did so on legs that threatened to wobble.

Tristan had danced himself into a sweat and abandoned his jacket, tossing it into the booth. Zoey noted that his shirt had a strategic amount of shirttail not tucked into his pants. She found it unlikely that he came upon the carelessly casual look by accident.

Zoey sat back down and fanned her face, blaming her glistening forehead on the excursion on the dance floor. Ruth and her friends were well into the festivities and there was little room left at the table. College guy had called over his wingman, and the table was littered with glasses as the server tried in vain to keep up with clearing the empties. Zoey didn't dare look directly at Tristan for fear he would be able to read her thoughts, but she could feel him watching her. She reached for a random champagne glass she hoped was hers and took a sip, peering at him momentarily from above the rim. Tristan's attention was diverted when Abbie grabbed his arm and dragged him back to the dance floor. He continued to dance with anyone who asked, and Zoey went back to watching. This time though she no longer felt any unexplained animosity as she did so. It turned out his full attention was more than she could handle. A strange role reversal, worrying about herself instead of him.

Ruth continued to dance the night away, alternating between Tristan, college guy, wingman, and several of Blake's fellow bachelor partyers, who had joined Blake when he made his way down from the party on the second floor of the club upon spotting her.

"Come on." Ruth literally tried to pull Blake onto the dance floor to no avail. "Loosen up that tie and let's get this party started."

Blake didn't budge from where he was standing. With a slight shake of his head and a knowing look, he took a sip from the bottle of beer he was holding.

"Don't worry, sexy lady, I got my boogie shoes on." One of Blake's friends, who'd been introduced as Randy, got between them. "Let's show the man what he's missing."

Ruth blew Blake a little kiss and grabbed Randy's hand. He lifted his arm, gave Ruth a twirl, and they went off to the dance floor.

Zoey liked Blake well enough, even if he was, at times, too serious. The girls often teased him about his RBF—Resting Brood Face. He was an odd addition to Ruth's circle of zaniness. Zoey had never seen him out of a suit and tie, no matter the weather, and tonight was no exception. He was the observe-and-analyze type, with iron self-control. The same could not be said for his friends. They were older and boisterous, openly evaluating the women in the bar, blatantly looking them up and down, going so far as to point out their attributes and flaws. Unsurprisingly, all their ring fingers were bare. Zoey wondered if they had slipped off the wedding rings to get a little side action. Ruth wasn't particular about who joined the party. Once again, Zoey's sister was holding court.

"Nice to see you, Zoey," Blake said when the music died down. She got up from where she was sitting to join him. "It's been a while since you've come out on a Saturday night."

"About as long as it's been since you've seen a dance floor?" she teased. She didn't want to tell the tale of Tristan. The way Tristan was acting, dancing, smiling, and carrying on, no one would believe he was a shy computer nerd.

"A crowded dance floor is no place for a guy with two left feet," he replied with his own brand of humor. "Not with everyone having a cell phone set to RECORD."

His excuse was a valid one. Zoey had seen Blake dance before, in the early days when he was eager to fit in, and he was not in Tristan's league.

At precisely one forty-five, Tristan began to make his good nights and good-byes. Through the chorus of urging him to stay, he merely smiled and politely declined. He told Ruth and her friends to enjoy the rest of the night—the tab was already taken care of. He turned to Zoey and asked, "Are you ready to go?"

He could've ended the question with anything. Get a tattoo, have something to eat, jump off the Verrazzano-Narrows Bridge, her answer would be the same. She would go with him anywhere. With a nod of her head and a wave to the table, she picked up her handbag, and together they made for the exit.

The cold air when they took their first step out the front door was welcome and invigorating. Wall-to-wall people working up a sweat made for the kind of stifling heat that the air-conditioning couldn't keep up with. Zoey noticed there was still a line of people waiting to get inside. She leaned her head back and took a deep inhale.

"The car is supposed to be here at two," Tristan said with a glance at the row of cars in front of the building. "We may be a few minutes early."

"Enjoy the rest of your weekend, kids."

Zoey turned around to the voice behind her and saw Blake approaching them. She was surprised. He had followed them out.

"You're leaving already?" Zoey asked. "The night is still young in there."

"I've been on and off a party bus since three o'clock this afternoon. It may be selfish, but I wanted to make my getaway before the puking started. Scraping the groom off the floor is the best man's job. I'm not even in the wedding party."

"Can we give you a lift?" Tristan offered. "I have a car coming."

"No thanks," Blake said. "I'm not going that far."

They watched Blake's back as he walked off into the shadows.

"You looked like you had fun tonight," she said to Tristan, still refraining from looking at him straight on or for too long.

"I did!" was his cheerful response. Then he turned deadly serious. "Now I have to ask you. Abbie told me to look her up on Tinder after I got rid of you. She said something about 'totally swiping me right.' Do you have any idea what she's talking about?"

Zoey had no desire to hold a grudge against Abbie. By all rights, Tristan was fair game. She had less of a desire to explain the ins and outs of Tinder to him. And while she had no problem being magnanimous, she wasn't batshit crazy.

"It means she's a free Veronica."

"Oh." His eyebrows arched in alarm. "I don't want any part of that."

"I didn't think so."

"Your sister is completely different from you."

A bubble of laughter escaped. "She certainly is her own woman. Derek calls her Ruthless."

With one sentence, Zoey had managed to ruin the night herself. Without thinking, she had brought up her husband. She was able to refrain from literally slamming her palm into her forehead, but mentally she gave herself quite a whack.

Tristan looked back at the bar and made a face. His concern returned. "Those guys were moving in pretty close to your sister. Do you think we did the right thing leaving her?"

"I have always been worried about Ruth and her shenanigans. But she always lands on her feet. You should be way more concerned that she's going to use your generosity to buy drinks for the entire bar."

"They don't have my credit card. If she can manage to spend all the cash I gave them, more power to her. But some of those guys she was dancing with looked creepy. The way one of them was staring at her backside made me want to punch him square in the nose."

Zoey laughed again, a little relieved. Tristan had been too preoccupied with chivalrous distraction to pick up on her slip of bringing up Derek. "You would've only robbed her of the pleasure of clobbering him herself. That is one woman who has no problem making it known she can take on all opponents. She once stabbed a guy with her car key. He needed seven stitches and still asked her out again."

The car pulled up, ending the conversation. And though she was loath to say the words, Zoey gave the driver her address to drop her off first, since her apartment was closer. This time, instead of looking out at the city during the silent drive, she snuck peeks at Tristan's profile as he watched the scenery through the windshield. His head was slightly swaying to the music the driver was playing. A delighted grin tugged at Tristan's lips, the evidence he had indeed enjoyed himself. He started to turn toward Zoey and she snapped her head forward just in time to keep from being caught watching him.

"I had a wonderful time tonight," he said softly. "I couldn't have done this without you. Thanks, Zoey."

She should've been proud, even if he was exaggerating. He didn't look like it took too much effort to get him relaxed. She had done what she set out to do, help him conquer another hurdle in his wish to really appreciate all the best things in life. But the only thought that was drumming in her head was that another magical night was over. Another night with a perfect gentleman. A needle in a haystack. A needle she unfortunately had found a little too late.

In too short a ride, the car pulled up in front of her building. Tristan stopped the driver from getting out to open her door and asked him to wait. He got out and ran around to her side to do it himself and walked her to the door.

"I'd like to walk you to your apartment," he said in a tone that brooked no argument. "Just in case some vagrant is hanging around the halls."

They got to the door of her apartment, and it was an awkward moment. The kind of moment that, if they weren't on different paths that somehow collided, would end in a kiss. She looked at his lips, watching them move.

"Thanks again, Zoey. Have a good night."

Unable to stop herself, she reached out her arms and wrapped them around his neck, giving him a tight squeeze. "You're welcome, Tristan. Good night."

At first his arms remained stiffly at his sides, but she couldn't bring herself to pull back and away. Then she felt first his arm then his hands draw lightly over her hips to settle around her waist as he awkwardly hugged her back.

Chapter 11

The last time Zoey was so restless was before she'd left Ohio for New York. She tossed and turned for hours in bed as the entire evening rewound in her memory. From the intimate discussion over the dinner Tristan had cooked for her, to the open looks of hunger from other women in the club, to his smoldering eyes on the dance floor and the hug he was too considerate to rebuff. She had only wanted to help him. Now she wished they could just hook up and get it out of the way. Break the tension so she could go back to grinding away at work instead of checking her phone a hundred times a day, in the hopes that he'd texted. The single silver lining of the night was that she couldn't recall having smiled once. There were sultry looks and pouting, but her secret neon gums were effectively concealed from Ruth and her crowd.

As soon as Zoey was done admonishing herself, a little voice inside her head would speak up. It would tell her how in just a few months, if all went according to plan, she'd be divorced. But then her logical side would counter that Tristan had never actually expressed an interest in her. There was no way of knowing where he stood without flat out asking him. When she got to questioning whether it would be worth the risk of ruining the friendship, the debate would start all over again.

It felt like she had just fallen asleep when Ruth shook her awake.

She didn't need to ask Ruth if she was just getting in. Ruth usually stayed out all night on Saturday, sometimes bringing the party back home. Letting Zoey have the bedroom on the weekends was mutually beneficial. Ruth was still wearing the same clothes, but her silky hair was now flat, her makeup all but gone, and her smoky eyeliner looked smeared. Her voice sounded giddy and a little buzzed. Ruth was always able to hold her liquor without stumbling. She had likely danced most of it off.

"What are you doing home?" Ruth asked.

Zoey sat up in bed and rubbed her face. "Where am I supposed to be?"

"I figured you went home with Mr. Good-boy."

Ruth gave a smug snort. "I told Abbie he was never going to get in touch."

Zoey's jaw tightened with the reminder of Abbie's invitation for Tristan to join her on Tinder. After last night, all her good will toward other women had come to a screeching halt.

"I told you he wasn't that kind of guy," she said irritably.

"Yeah," Ruth continued to scoff. "You also told me he was a nerd and looked like a baby duck. That was a boldface lie. That man is scrumptious."

"He's not for you." Zoey issued the warning.

"Of course he's not!" This time Ruth added a laugh. "He's way too square and noble for me. I'm more the bad-boy-aching-to-be-tamed type."

"What's the matter, none of those available last night?" Zoey wanted to talk about Tristan. Ask if Ruth noticed him staring at her with longing or displaying some sudden outburst of jealousy. Anything to suggest that he was harboring feelings for her. But Zoey knew her sister. Ruth was all about Ruth. If it didn't concern her, or you didn't specifically send out an SOS, it didn't hold her interest.

"It was an off night." Ruth yawned and kicked off her shoes. Zoey lay back down and Ruth curled up beside her, just as she had when they were kids. "Once Blake left, his bachelor party friends all became animals. One of them grabbed a handful of my ass near the end of the night. I kneed him in the nuts before the bouncers tossed him out. They didn't show me the door, since I was the offended party, but they did make it clear it was time for us to call it a night. We all went out for breakfast. I think Erin and Abbie took those young guys home."

Zoey giggled. Nothing sends a message that this girl isn't worth it quite like watching a fellow comrade falling to his knees with his hands covering his groin. For all her faults, Ruth was true to her own code of conduct. Look all you want, but don't touch her unless invited. Thank goodness they had already left. Tristan might've thought he'd landed on a reality show.

"It was nice of Tristan to pick up the tab," Ruth murmured drowsily. "Please thank him for us. Did you have fun?"

Before Zoey could make up her mind how best to answer, she heard Ruth's breathing change to deep and nasal. In typical Ruth fashion, she had fallen asleep before Zoey could respond. She should've known the question was rhetorical, Zoey mused, closing her eyes again as well.

The next time Zoey woke up, it was four hours later and she was still tired. She eased herself out of bed, careful not to disturb Ruth, threw on some clothes, and went down to the corner. Sundays when she didn't have a job were spent with coffee and bagels from the local café followed by being lazy and binge-watching Netflix or playing on iPads. If Ruth was feeling up to snuff, they might have dinner at one of the hundred restaurants within walking distance. If Ruth was feeling wrecked, they called for takeout.

Zoey's body may have gotten the lazy message, but her mind was having no part of it. It swirled in a storm of indecision. It was the same sort of pattern that she had adopted when things got rough with Derek, when she went to bed every night with a lump in her throat and a twist in her gut. She didn't like it, and she was the only one who could make it stop. It was time to start making her own needs paramount again. The problem with her line of thinking was, she wasn't sure what her needs were anymore.

She had accomplished breaking Tristan out of his shell. He didn't have a disability and he wasn't a child that needed to be babysat. She didn't need to hold his hand through every step of his journey. The only flaw in that logic was that she very much wanted to hold his hand. And kiss his full, sometimes pouty lips. And rip off all the fancy new clothes she helped him acquire. She could also call Derek and tell him that she was sorry, but she didn't want to wait the extra time and she had decided to act now. If she was thinking about another man, the marriage was surely over regardless. But going back on her word left her with a rotten taste in her mouth. And a two-month chaste courtship would be right up Tristan's alley anyway.

Ruth dragged herself out of bed around noon. She came down the hall on autopilot, microwaved her cold coffee, and covered a bagel with cream cheese, making intermittent groans. She collapsed on the futon, next to Zoey.

"I need to talk to you," Zoey tentatively began. "About Tristan."

"I knew it!" Ruth's sluggishness evaporated and she perked right up. Apparently Zoey's crisis of confidence was better than a cup of coffee. "Did you let him down easy?"

"Wait. What are you talking about?"

"What are you talking about? You did tell him about Derek, right?"

Maybe this wasn't such a good idea. In her jumbled state, Zoey had forgotten Ruth's fondness for Derek.

"I'm the one who has feelings for Tristan. Not the other way around. I can't tell if he finds me desirable, and I'm scared to tell him."

"But you did tell him that you're married?" Ruth repeated.

"Yes, not long after we met. It's the main reason I'm in this quandary now. You and Derek talking me into this stupid agreement. Tristan is too proper to make any sort of move with me while I'm still attached to someone else. But if I wait, I'm going to miss my chance. And if I'm wrong altogether, I'm setting myself up for heartbreak."

Ruth chewed her bagel and Zoey waited with growing impatience for her to weigh in.

"I think the first thing you should do is wait for him to make contact. Do *not* contact him, for any reason. He's not the kind to play hard to get, so if he's interested, he'll reach out sooner rather than later."

Zoey picked up the other half of her sister's bagel and took a bite, more out of nervous habit than hunger. This idea already stunk. Before last night, she didn't have to worry about him getting in touch. In fact, he texted so often, he was on the border of becoming a nuisance. After last night, it all felt different. Everything had changed. "And if he never makes contact?"

Ruth gave an uncharacteristically sympathetic shake of her head. "Then you have your answer, even if it's one you don't like."

Zoey began to grimace. "And if he does reach out?"

"If he texts, it's easy. Be cordial, friendly, stick with your usual banter. The idea here is to keep both of you from coming up against that wall until the year is over. You don't want to burn either bridge until you're sure. If you go back to Derek, none of it will matter, because you'll be on your way back to Cleveland."

Zoey didn't know how to express what her gut told her—the decision had already been made. She had fallen for Tristan. But right now, she needed her sister's help, not to get into a useless argument with her.

"And what if Tristan calls?"

Ruth gave that angle a tad more thought. "That's easy too. Just let it go to voice mail for a couple days. It'll buy you more time. Then, when you do pick up, if he's calling just to chat, you have to run. You're on your way to a job. You make it quick but cheery."

"What if he's calling me to do a job?"

"Only you can make the call about that one. That's business. And he has no problem opening his wallet. Turning him down would be cutting your nose off to spite your face. But then you have every reason to act professionally instead of chummy. See the pattern here? The key is getting him to make a move."

"I don't want to hurt him," Zoey said, hating every bit of what Ruth was telling her. Their friendship was based on honesty. All of this ducking and diving reeked of deceit.

"Zoe, there's a broken heart for every light on Broadway. He has money, he has looks, all the resources to help him get over it. He'll find another friend to fawn over him."

Suddenly Zoey regretted not telling Ruth the full story. About just how wholesome and uncorrupted he actually was. What a mess he was when she met him. That his only lover had been a call girl he was too naive to spot. Not that her sister would believe her after last night. Ruth would just accuse her of being oversensitive and sentimental.

"And if it turns out he feels the same way I do?"

"Hey, girl," Ruth said with a smile. "I can't dictate your life story for you. That one I'm staying out of. You are on your own there."

Ruth resumed eating her bagel and sipping her coffee. Zoey went back to daydreaming. Then Ruth spoke up again, with her final thoughts on the matter.

"I don't much see the point in all of this anyway. You know you're going to go back to Derek. You guys have been together since you were kids. You two are lifers."

Zoey hoped it was just coincidence that *lifers* was the word for people stuck in prison forever.

Chapter 12

Nobody expects an uninvited knock on their door on a Sunday evening. When Zoey looked through the peephole and saw two blue uniforms, she feared the worst. Someone was dead.

"Is this the residence of Ruth Dixon?" the older of the two asked, double-checking the name on the paper he was holding.

They didn't have guns drawn, but it also didn't look like a social call.

"I'm her," Ruth said, getting up from the couch. She didn't look like she expected them either.

"We have a warrant for your arrest, miss."

"A what?" Zoey and Ruth said in unison.

They didn't look like the cops you saw in the movies, all grizzled and by the book. These cops were more relaxed. Official-looking, but more like they were running an errand, not making an apprehension. The police handed over the piece of paper they had brought with them. Ruth scanned the document for the key words. It was easy to see when she got the gist by how pale she turned and her hands started to shake.

"I'm being arrested for assault. From that perv last night in the bar!"

"I don't think we have to cuff her," the younger cop said, and the older cop gave a single nod.

"I don't think you understand. He assaulted me first!" Ruth's pale face was replacing itself with a flush of anger. She handed over the warrant for Zoey to read.

"You can tell your side to the judge. We don't want to use the handcuffs on you, if you're willing to just come along with us. And you can make it easier for everyone if you leave all your valuables behind."

"The offense you're talking about is a misdemeanor. Aren't there actual crimes that you guys could be dealing with? You know, murders, muggers . . . ," Zoey tried to point out.

"We don't make the rules, miss, we enforce them. They consider assault a felony when the victim is a federal employee, in this case a judge. Rumor has it when he swore out the complaint, he was taking it personally. The bouncers in the bar weren't very gentle."

Only Ruth would try teaching a hands-off lesson to a judge.

"This is ridiculous," Zoey said, crumpling up the warrant when fisting her hand. She started to try and undo the damage by flattening it against the wall and hand ironing it. "A complete abuse of power."

"I don't know what I'm supposed to do here." Ruth looked down at her grungy Sunday sweatpants and black tank top, an attempt for normalcy as it started to sink in. "Can I change?"

The cops exchanged glances. The older one gave a half nod. "What you have on is perfect for jail. It's not going to be like a night at the Ritz. We'll let you grab another shirt. It gets cold. They probably won't uniform you up. It'll take most of the night to process you. You'll be arraigned first thing tomorrow morning. We'll wait right here. Just don't close the door."

"You do have the right to remain silent." The young cop started reciting her Miranda rights as Ruth took off down the hall.

Ruth went to get a sweatshirt while the cops waited inside the open doorway. Zoey followed closely behind into the bedroom.

"Oh, my God." Ruth started pulling shirts out of drawers in search of her most comfortable one. "I'm going to spend a night in jail."

"What do you want me to do?" Zoey said.

"I don't even know what I'm going to do. But if I get an inkling, I'll call you. I do get to make one phone call, right?"

"I feel like I'm supposed to come with you or something," Zoey fretted.

"Unless you're going to spend the night staging a protest outside, there's no point in that."

"Do you know any lawyers? Do you want me to call Blake?"

"I want you to call them all, but I get the feeling it's not going to do any good right now. I can't believe the nerve of this guy. Right now, my only regret is not kicking him harder."

"Ruth, now is not the time to go all balls to the wall. This is one of those situations where apologizing would go a long way. You can plot his demise after you get out and lawyer up."

"This is a nightmare," Ruth said, taking one last look at herself in the mirror as the reality hit her full force. She gave herself a quick finger comb.

"They're waiting," Zoey said quietly.

"There is something you can do," Ruth said, her voice shaky. "Call work for me in the morning? Tell them I'm sick, can't stop throwing up. That's not far from the truth."

The cops led Ruth down the small hall to the stairs and away. The apartment, despite the television still being on, now seemed eerily quiet. Zoey started to pace from room to room. She picked up and put down her phone half a dozen times, resisting the urge to call Tristan. She picked up her phone one last time, this time to place a call. To Derek.

"Hey, baby," he greeted her. "I was just thinking about you."

"They just hauled Ruth off to jail," she blurted. "I don't know what the hell I should be doing!"

Normally, his chuckling was aggravating. This time, it lent an air of feeling that everything was going to be all right. "Oh shit, Ruthless must've really messed up if she wasn't able to talk herself out of it."

Zoey told Derek the story of her night with Ruth and the handsy judge. She left out any mention of Tristan.

"I don't think this guy would want to take it all the way. A good defense attorney would make him look like a pervert, and that's rotten publicity whether it's true or not. Sounds like he's trying to prove a point."

"Like what? That he has great power at his disposal and he uses it to crush women who aren't interested in him?"

"That. Or maybe he doesn't appreciate a kick in

the jewels. She'll probably get a fine, maybe some community service."

"Don't forget a criminal record!" Zoey said hotly. This was serious. Ruth was behind bars. "Dixons are a lot of things, but we aren't jailbirds!"

"You aren't a Dixon anymore." Derek, as usual, took the most inopportune moment to get back to his agenda. "You're a Sullivan. You should be grateful you aren't sitting in that cell with her."

"Derek, please don't make me regret reaching out to you."

"I'm sorry. I can't help it. But when you call me late on a Sunday night to tell me your sister just went to jail for losing her cool after a night of partying, I have to worry. You've been cleaning up after your sister's misadventures since we all were kids. You can't fix her and she doesn't want to be saved. I'm afraid you're going to get caught up in one of her messes."

So much of what he said was the truth. But Derek wasn't known for his timing. Zoey's response was silence followed by a long, drawn-out sigh. Before hanging up, Derek left her with one more attempt at comforting.

"Look, Ruth is going to be fine. She's going to spend a night in jail, something that in the long run might do her some good. There's nothing you can do for her between now and the morning, so get some sleep tonight and then just go pick her up."

After the second night in a row spent tossing and turning, Zoey had barely fallen asleep when she was awakened right after sunrise by another pounding on the front door. Luckily, this time when she looked through the peephole, she saw Ruth's eye up close, blinking back at her from the other side.

Zoey opened the door with a sigh of relief. Her sister didn't look too worse for wear, other than the dark circles under her eyes.

"That was harrowing," Ruth said while breezing in and flopping down on the futon.

"How did you get out so soon? They said last night you wouldn't be arraigned until this morning."

"It's all about who you know." After all she'd been through, Ruth still was able to appear haughty.

"I'm too tired to play guessing games or congratulate you on your network of friends. Just answer the question."

"I would've picked up coffee," Ruth continued, "but as you know, I left here without my wallet."

"We can make coffee. Are you still in trouble or what?"

"I probably could've gotten the guys at the bagel place to front me a couple of cups, but it'd be over my dead body that I'd let them see me dressed like this."

"RUTH!!" Zoey's already frayed nerves had reached their breaking point.

"Okay!" Ruth laughed. "I knew a couple of detectives at the station. They were just as surprised as I was, since not once did they ever tell me they were cops. Or maybe they did and I just forgot."

"Ruth," Zoey repeated, this time as a growl.

"Relax! While they were booking me, these guys intervened. I never saw the inside of a jail cell. They called and woke up a judge they knew, who didn't take kindly to having an already overextended justice system being burdened by the hurt feelings of an out-of-town traffic court judge. They couldn't get me out of the court date, but they were able to spring me on my own recognizance. And I scored a date for the fireworks on the Fourth of July, on a boat in the harbor, no less."

Sometimes Ruth's free spirit and the way she ranked her priorities were enough to make Zoey homicidal.

"So, this guy isn't even a judge for New York City?"

"He's not even a resident of the state. Lives and works in some sleepy little town in New Jersey. Allenhurst?

Allenwood? Allentown?" Ruth gave a dismissive wave of her hand. "Something Allen, I forget."

No wonder Zoey was often tired. Ruth was exhausting. Why be bothered with retaining the pertinent information regarding the man who wanted to put you in jail when you can line up a date for something three months away?

"I did find out the judge's last name is Hollister. Randolph Hollister. Even his name sounds uptight."

What Zoey should've done was remind Ruth that she wasn't out of the woods yet, that this man was still gunning for her. But she settled on "What are you going to do now?"

Ruth stood up and took off her sweatshirt. "Right now, I'm going to go take a Silkwood shower. That police precinct was grungy as hell. Did you call work for me?"

Zoey shook her head, dumbfounded. "It's barely daylight. I was going to wait for HR to open."

"That's okay," Ruth said, heading for the hallway. "I'll call them myself. I need a day off. Why don't you get dressed and grab us some coffee? And breakfast. I'm starving."

Zoey watched her sister stroll out of the room, resisting the urge to jump out of her chair, run down the hall, and commit a sneak-up strangulation. Why was Ruth always able to adopt a laissez-faire attitude? An even better question was, how could Zoey become more like her?

After a shower and some clean clothes, Ruth returned to the living room. She curled up next to Zoey on the futon, laying her head on Zoey's shoulder. Ruth had been more rattled by the whole ordeal than she was letting on.

"Maybe you should call Blake?" Zoey suggested, breaking the silence.

"Maybe" was Ruth's response.

Why was Ruth hesitant?

"Chances are if Randolph Hollister was part of the bachelor party, Blake is going to get wind of the story anyway."

"Then I guess I won't need to call him," Ruth said with a yawn. "I'll be getting his advice whether I want it or not."

"Why don't you want to get Blake's advice? He has to have some tips."

Ruth gave a heavy sigh. "Because he would jump right in to try and save the day, usually with some well-meaning lecture at the end. About how if I would cut back on the partying and take myself seriously, I could really be going places. And he would refuse to take money, which would piss me off all the more."

If Zoey had half a brain, she would steal Ruth's phone and make the call herself. Currently she wasn't feeling strong enough to withstand Ruth's wrath for butting in. The mere way Ruth said "piss me off" was enough to make her cringe.

"Oh, the horror," Zoey said instead. "A nice, handsome guy that's actually a good friend and wants the best for you. I can see where that would cause a problem."

"Now you're getting it." Ruth laughed weakly. She paused, then added, "Blake is a great guy, but he's a doofus. He never dances. He drinks only bottled beer that he has to watch the bartender open 'cause he's worried someone will slip him a Mickey. And believe me when I tell you, he never puts that bottle down unless it's right in front of him."

Not drinking random liquids poured into glasses and left alone in crowded nightclubs didn't seem stupid to Zoey—it sounded downright logical.

"And those suits!" Ruth continued, having built up a full head of steam. "I mean seriously, who wears a damn suit to go to the movies? Or bowling?"

"Only you could take issue with a man who likes to wear a suit."

"Abbie and Erin swear this summer they are inviting him to the beach to see what he shows up in. His legs are probably all pasty white."

"Haven't all of you seen him without his suit? I mean, even you hooked up with him once."

"I have to admit; his birthday suit is fine," Ruth conceded before adding, "but the sex was so polite. 'Is touching you here all right? Are you sure about this?' I'm one step from coming all over the place and he's asking me if I'm having a good time. Maddening."

There was nothing left for Zoey to say. Blake had done exactly what every man is supposed to do. But Ruth would never understand that if she didn't already. What Blake apparently didn't understand was that if Ruth didn't like something, not only would he know it, but everyone for an entire city block would know it as well.

Chapter 13

Zoey refused to sit on the sidelines and watch the crisis with Ruth play itself out. She looked up all the courts in New Jersey and the judges who presided over them until she found Randolph Hollister. While Ruth was at work the following day, Zoey took the train to New Jersey and a cab to the courthouse where Randolph Hollister was officiating over Tuesday's traffic court. She sat among the sea of scofflaws and lawyers waiting their turns to plead out on speeding tickets and running red lights. It was a huge line of the guilty and the presumed innocent. She waited, then stood with everyone else when the bailiff called the court to order.

Without the club lighting, the throbbing beats, and the frenzied dancing, the questionably Honorable

Randolph Hollister cut quite the dashing figure, right down to the wedding ring he was now wearing. The robe made him look way more dignified than the goofy dude on the dance floor, trying to make the most of the two steps he knew. Before he was just another schlub in the club making moony eyes at her sister and laughing at his own pickup lines. When you take people out of their context, they appear differently, something Zoey realized she should've figured out by now. Lesson learned. Again.

Zoey wasn't sure how to approach him and what she'd say when and if she got the chance. She watched as he delivered the same monologue time after time, asking what their crime was and if they willingly entered their plea, and saying what the typical sentence was for each offense. Then he'd rattle off their fine and the court costs and it would be on to the next person.

He was empathetic in his dealings with the people who stood before him, even matter-of-fact in his delivery. He didn't go off on long tangents at the litigants. He waited as long as he could before he issued bench warrants for people who didn't show up to answer their summonses, calling out their names with a quick look around the room, before finally handing off the paperwork to his clerk.

Zoey knew he recognized her when during one of his scans of the courtroom, his gaze rested on her and he did a double take. Then he looked directly at her and his stare turned icy. The whole encounter took less than three seconds, but it was enough to make her blood run cold through her veins.

This is a huge mistake, Zoey thought. She watched, glued to her seat near the back of the room, as the judge became less and less tolerant of the defendants that stood before him. Fines began increasing and sentences became stiffer, accompanied by stinging lectures about responsibility, and he barked orders of silence when people tried to explain themselves. All done with intermittent glares in her direction.

After one of those scowls, Judge Hollister motioned to the bailiff by crooking a finger. The bailiff bent his head toward the judge while covering the court microphone with his hand. They shared a muted exchange and they both looked at her. When the bailiff headed toward where she was sitting, Zoey's flight response kicked in. She jumped out of her seat and out the closest door.

She ran until her chest hurt when she tried to draw breath and the pain in her side was unbearable, her legs turning into cramp-filled logs. She slowed down to a hurried walk back to the train station.

Safely on the train back to the city, Zoey was unable to quell the shudders that continued to plague her. It would've been one thing if Randolph Hollister was nasty and abrupt to everyone, but until he caught sight of her, he seemed logical and compassionate. He knew he was no innocent victim when it came to what happened with Ruth. One look at her was all it took for him to have what she considered a public temper tantrum. And that made Zoey feel worse. Thanks to her efforts, all she managed to accomplish was doubling the fine for a guy with an expired insurance card and a woman receiving a ten-minute scolding about how she shouldn't be speeding with kids in the car.

"Of all the arrogant, pigheaded, sanctimonious . . . ," Ruth sputtered after Zoey reported the news.

At least she wasn't angry at Zoey for trying to approach him on her behalf. She waited patiently for Ruth to settle into a more obscenity-laced tirade. Ruth could swear better than the average sailor on shore leave.

"You know what?" Ruth threw her Lean Cuisine dinner into the microwave and slammed the door. "I had no idea that the bouncers face-planted him on the street, and if he wasn't such a first-rate ass clown I would almost feel sorry for him."

"What are you going to do?" Zoey asked.

Ruth watched her sesame chicken spin around in the microwave. Zoey could practically hear the wheels turning as Ruth considered her options. She turned back to Zoey with an evil smile.

"I'm not going to do anything."

"You're not going to show up to court?" Zoey was aghast.

"Oh, I'm going to show up to court all right. And I'm going to show up looking like the most innocent, proper damsel they ever saw."

"Don't you think your money would be better spent in hiring a lawyer instead?" Zoey longed to introduce Blake back into the conversation. If nothing else, he would give her good advice.

"I wasn't going to buy anything. I thought maybe I could borrow some of your clothes?"

If Zoey wasn't so apprehensive of where Ruth was going with this, the insult might have stung more. "I don't own anything like that. And we are not even remotely the same size. You mean you're going to go for the baggy matron look?"

Ruth briefly looked Zoey up and down. "You're right. Looks like I'm going shopping."

"You need to be shopping for an attorney."

"I'm not throwing away money to try and fight a rigged system," Ruth scoffed.

Zoey was nibbling on her cuticles—a bad habit that she thought she'd beaten years ago. "I think that's a bad idea."

"Which is why you're you and I'm me. I'm going to make this joker look like the worst kind of creeper."

The verdict was in. Ruth was going insane. She was going to go full throttle against someone Zoey had just explained was a first-class jerk. Explaining to his wife what happened to him that night must have been quite inconvenient for him. Randolph Hollister didn't seem like a man who would let go of a grudge. From all she had witnessed, she seriously had to question if he even had a moral code. Ruth was a force to be reckoned with, but he had a much better arsenal. Zoey knew where her loyalty had to lie, but it didn't mean she was at all comfortable with it.

After sending a text to Tristan asking if she could stop by and seeing his warm reception to her text, Zoey grabbed her purse and left, without another word.

Chapter 14

Zoey made one stop before getting to Tristan's. When he answered the door, he was back in his goofy golf clothes, this time red plaid knickers that tucked into his white knee-high socks and a white polo shirt. Given the recent turn of events, they, and he, were a sight for sore eyes.

"I didn't want to miss you, so I was waiting to clean up until you got here," he said, reaching for the shopping bags she carried. "I was starting to think you had changed your mind."

"Not a chance," Zoey replied excitedly. "I just got an idea and made a pit stop. To thank you for the other night. Take those to the living room."

On the way over to his apartment, she had thought about telling him about Ruth's latest escapade, then decided against it. She was tired of Ruth. She needed a break from the stress of it. After remembering how Tristan released stress, she got an idea. Zoey made a small detour to the GameStop.

"Zoey," Tristan said, pulling the guitar out of the bag by its long neck. "I think your guitar is missing some strings. Like all of them."

"No, it's not." She laughed. "I remembered what you said about Sonic the Hedgehog. I figured it was time to get your gaming into the twenty-first century."

And if he was going to like it as much as she was thinking he would, it would curtail some of his television watching. She pulled the used gaming console out of the box, complete with cables already plugged in. "This is a PlayStation Three. Sorry I had to buy one used. The new ones are a little out of my budget. And if you hate it, then I can say I tried and not feel awful."

"I've heard of these," he said with fascination, still staring at the black plastic guitar with its colorful buttons on the neck and lever used to strum. "But all the commercials have them being used for games where you shoot people. Or steal cars while shooting people. Then you team up with other players and shoot people. They look too violent for me."

"Not all of them, my friend," she replied while pulling the final object out of the bag, a DVD case. "This game is called Guitar Hero. And don't worry, you can play it alone without being noticed by anybody else's system. There are a whole bunch of versions, but I picked out the one that is all Aerosmith."

"You didn't." They exchanged grins, remembering the night they met.

"Don't get too excited. I'm not sure 'Walk This Way' is on the playlist."

Their grins turned into full-blown smiles.

"Come on, techno guy, let's figure out how to plug this thing into your television and get to rocking."

Between the two of them, they were able to hook up the console without directions. When they were done, he picked up the guitar and held it out to her. "You want to do the honors?"

Zoey shook her head. "No way, this is your toy. But I'd be willing to pick the song."

Excited to get started, they skipped the tutorial. She chose "Sweet Emotion." "Now remember, the colored stars coincide with the colors on the frets. You push the colors and strum with that lever where the hole in a normal guitar would be."

Tristan flicked at the thin metal arm that extended out from the guitar. "What the heck does this thing do?"

"I think that's called a whammy bar. It's for when you want to riff like crazy. But one thing at a time, okay?" She pushed the button to start the game and raced to the couch for a front-row seat to his first concert.

"What am I supposed to do about all those people standing in front of the stage?" He pointed to the television as the music keyed up.

"They're your crowd, waiting for the show to start."

"Amazing."

And in his plaid golf knickers, he proceeded to butcher "Sweet Emotion." He started out well enough. When he blew that first chord, he winced like he'd been electrocuted. The virtual crowd let out a yell of discontent. Then it turned into pure torture to her ears. His fingers struggled to keep up as the stars moved faster across the television screen. Some of his sour notes created such a screech, Zoey waited for the glass in the windows to shatter. By the time the game labeled him a total failure and the crowd rained down their disapproval, the other players in his band throwing down their instruments to walk away in disgust, Zoey and Tristan were both laughing so hard, they were wiping away tears.

"That was awful!" He fell down onto the couch beside her.

"Cringe worthy," she agreed when she finally caught her breath, still clutching her sides.

"I think that audience called me a lot of things. Hero wasn't one of them."

"Yeah, they were a tough crowd. I think your bandmates stormed off to have a meeting and fire you."

Tristan refused to be daunted. Zoey kept picking songs and he kept trying to play them. Her attempts fared no better. Plus, it was much more fun to watch him. He was so engrossed, he never bothered to change out of his golf attire, which added to her overall enjoyment. Somewhere around midnight, they had a pizza delivered, another first for him.

"You know," he said sincerely, after tearing into his third slice of Ray's Works, "Guitar Hero and pizza may be the best things that ever happened to me. Next to you, that is."

She wished he wouldn't do that. Look at her that way, with the big wide eyes and disarming smile. Say things that were borderline what a lover would say, even though she knew he always spoke from the heart. Zoey concentrated on her pizza.

"Is it corny to say that's music to my ears?" she said.

"Maybe, but I don't think there's enough corny nowadays. It's a welcome reprieve from sarcastic."

They played until almost three in the morning before Tristan said, "I hope you don't have to work tomorrow."

"Luckily, I'm off till the weekend." For the first time since she started being her own boss, she wasn't completely overexcited with taking another step in her adventure. In the moment, with an old worn-out Play-Station, a pizza, and Tristan was where she wanted to be. It was a strange reversal; instead of getting him out in the world, staying cloistered in his little part of it was infinitely better.

"That doesn't mean I don't have to start heading home."

"You're welcome to stay here," he offered. "You can take my bed. I'll sleep on the couch."

Hospitality was what he was raised on. There was nothing untoward in his invitation. Spontaneous sleepovers were for the friends who didn't mind it when they saw you with bedhead or sheet lines on your face or film on your teeth. Or who were going to see you naked, possibly misplace your panties.

"I appreciate the invite, but I have stuff to do first thing in the morning."

The words were barely out of her mouth and he was pulling the phone out of its cradle to call his car service.

Maybe he had second thoughts about the spontaneous invitation idea as well.

"There's no way I'm letting you go without making sure you get home safely," he said while dialing.

"Tomorrow I wouldn't mind picking up where we left off." she hedged, wanting to gauge his reaction.

He looked up from the phone and smiled. "It's a date."

Zoey came home to an empty apartment and fell asleep as soon as her head hit the pillow, too tired to worry about Ruth's whereabouts. She woke up briefly when Ruth got home to change for work. Ruth quietly went through her get-ready routine, their conversation little more than "good morning" and "have a good day," and Zoey fell back to sleep with the sound of the front door closing. The next time she opened her eyes, it was nearly noon and Tristan had texted he'd be home after two.

When she got to his place, added to the guitar was an additional guitar, an entire video game console drum kit, and a microphone complete with stand.

And he was wearing his leather pants. Those hot, delicious leather pants. A black ribbed tank top showed off his golfer's tan, cutting the color off midsinew on his biceps.

"What's all this?" Zoey asked, averting her eyes from him to keep from drooling.

"After you told me that Guitar Hero had lots of other versions, I went to check some of them out. That's when I learned there's a game called Rock Band. I couldn't resist getting the entire setup. Now we can play together."

There was no way for her to tell him that watching him had become her favorite game. She loved to watch the way his face scrunched up in concentration and how he unconsciously bit into his lower lip when he had to speed up his movements to keep from missing notes or a long drawn-out chord. Add all the leather and muscle, and it was a no-brainer.

"Tristan Malloy, I think you're obsessed." An easy statement for her to make, since it was how she felt as well. Only her obsession had nothing to do with music or silly video games.

"I'm not going to deny it. Did you know in the most recent versions, the crowd isn't quite so rude? The guys in the band still get pretty pissed though."

"What a bunch of divas."

"Do you want to play?" he asked, slinging the guitar strap over his shoulder.

The only playing she wanted to do with him had nothing to do with instruments. If she didn't know him better, she would swear he had begun to tease her.

"Sure." Zoey sat down at the drums and picked up the sticks. Not only did she want to spare him her singing, but she also thought it would be the easiest instrument to keep up with. It would also ensure that he was standing in front of her, so she could watch the leather pants in action. She tried to twirl one of the sticks between her fingers like a pro and promptly dropped it.

Tristan was a quick learner. Most of the booing was directed at Zoey's drumming skills. She missed most of her cues after any drum break she had because she was too busy watching him. She didn't feel the least bit guilty. They switched the instruments up here and there, with them both on guitars next to each other being Zoey's favorite.

When he moved over to the microphone and picked "Learn to Fly" from the Foo Fighters, Zoey was mesmerized. Not only did he have a lovely baritone, something he now felt comfortable enough to share, but he also felt free to add some of the dance moves she still had trouble erasing from her memory. Her opinion hadn't changed. She couldn't remember the last time she'd seen hips that swiveled like that. Tristan seemed to get off on the crowd cheering, going so far as to point at the TV screen as if they could see him. He knew the chorus without needing the words that scrolled across the screen and belted them out with his eyes closed. It was nothing short of adorable, and when he was done with the song Zoey realized she hadn't played a single note. Thankfully, Tristan had been so into his performance, he hadn't noticed her watching him.

"That was so fun," he remarked, sticking the microphone back in the stand.

"I have to go," Zoey said quickly, taking off the guitar. "I forgot I have some price quotes to work up."

It was an excuse, but the walls felt like they were closing in and she needed to get out of the room before she did something she'd regret.

Tristan looked confused.

"Oh. Okay," he said, trying to mask his disappointment. "I was going to make dinner tonight."

"I'm going to have to take a rain check. I'm late with these quotes as it is," she lied. She gathered up her things and hustled out the door, unable to look him in the eye.

Her feet dragged as she made her way back home. It seemed fitting. Her spirit had begun to drag as well. Maybe it was the lyrics to the Foo Fighters song, the symbolism she was mistakenly attaching to them—about looking for someone to save him—and the heartfelt way he sang them, the way he already knew most of the words. Maybe Ruth had been right all along, about the unlikelihood of being able to make a platonic friendship work. It didn't matter. There was no way around it.

She had fallen for Tristan Malloy.

Chapter 15

When Tristan called her the next day to chat, Zoey told him about what was happening with Ruth before he could extend any invitations. She stopped short of telling the part about her sister's ill-conceived idea to handle the situation without a lawyer. She was grateful that this time she had a valid excuse for telling him that the next few days were going to be busy.

"That guy was a judge? Wow. Is there anything I can do to help?"

His words and genuine concern were comforting, but all Zoey felt was stress. She had betrayed their friendship by falling for him. And now she was too scared and selfish to tell him for fear of him backing off. She was too drawn to him to have any hope of walking away herself.

"There's nothing for you to do, but thanks," she told him. Her voice was shaky, something that she hoped he'd interpret as worry.

"Do you want me to come along for support?" Tristan persisted in his desire to lend a hand. "I was there and can testify that he was buzzing around her all night."

"Hopefully, it won't get that far. But I hope that offer stands if it does."

"It certainly does. Good luck with all of it. Keep me posted?"

As Ruth got closer to her court appearance, her bravado started to nose-dive. Zoey accompanied Ruth on her shopping trip to transform herself into a prim schoolmarm. She wanted to make sure Ruth was dressed as conservatively as possible and be there to talk her out of wanting to wear something more Ruthie if she gravitated toward it. It was an eye-rolling ordeal.

"Is this made of polyester or sandpaper?"

"This is not cashmere. It feels more like dog hair."

"The neckline on this piece of crap is trying to strangle me."

"Are we trying to conceal my figure altogether?"

"I wonder if wearing this would entitle me to a senior citizen discount?"

Zoey bit her tongue and figured Ruth was lashing out, trying to hide her worry about her potential sentence. But she was also hurt. The majority of the garments Zoey selected she personally found attractive. As she presented countless armfuls of clothing that were ridiculed she reflected on two thoughts:

This wasn't half as fun as when she took Tristan to Barneys, and she remembered why she stopped shopping with her sister in the first place.

Ruth finally settled on a lovely three-quarter-length flower-patterned dress with a navy-blue cardigan that Ruth declared she would gladly donate to Zoey when she was done if it fit, which they both knew it wouldn't. Luckily their feet were within a size of each other's, which mercifully saved Zoey having to replay the whole rigmarole while shoe shopping too. Ruth was content to borrow a pair of plain black flats.

Neither of them had any appetite the morning of Ruth's hearing. The entire cab ride to the courthouse was an ongoing lecture of how Ruth needed to keep her mouth shut unless she was spoken to and to take whatever chip she had on her shoulder and brush it off now, before she came face-to-face with her accuser. Once they got to the courthouse and took a good look around, all of Ruth's defiance about raging against the machine came to a grinding halt. After going through the metal detectors, they found their courtroom and took their seats among a multitude of other grim and dazed faces. The people who didn't look fazed by what was going on around them were even more frightening. It was a real eclectic group of potential homicidal maniacs and their weary-looking public defenders. They waited as one by one defendants stood before the judge. Some of them were already wearing prison jumpsuits. Others were completely shackled as they shuffled their way to the front of the room to utter the one or two words required of them while their attorneys did the rest of the talking before being led back to wherever they came from. Some looked hopeless, others helpless. If they weren't so worried about the fate that awaited Ruth, they would've been depressed just being there. At times, Ruth grabbed Zoey's hand and gave it a squeeze. They waited as the process continued and there were only a handful of people left in the courtroom. They heard the judge call her case and Ruth went up to stand behind the defendant's table. At the same time, the prosecutor began searching through the amassed papers and folders that were stacked in front of him.

"Are you represented by counsel?" the judge asked Ruth.

"No, sir," Ruth replied.

"Are you waiving that right?"

"I'm throwing myself on the mercy of the court," Ruth said in all seriousness. The judge remained completely deadpan.

"If I may interject, Your Honor," the prosecutor chimed in with the paper he was looking for now in front of him. "The victim in this case no longer wants to press charges and we are recommending a dismissal."

"I have no record of that, counselor. Would you approach the bench, please? Bring your document with you."

The prosecutor did as he was asked while Ruth turned around to shrug her shoulders at Zoey. They exchanged puzzled looks and Zoey began to hold her breath. Maybe everything was going to be all right after all.

"Well, Miss Dixon," the judge began, and Ruth turned quickly back around, standing as straight as she could. "Looks like it's your lucky day. The injured party has rescinded his complaint, and per the prosecutor's recommendation, I'm going to dismiss your case. You're free to go."

"Thank you, Your Honor," Ruth said, the relief evident in her face.

The only sound that could be heard in the silence that followed as the judge updated his records was the whoosh of Zoey releasing her pent-up breath. Just like that, it was over and Ruth was joining her. Ruth's relief was apparently left at the defendant's table, replaced with an eye-rolling annoyance.

"Can you believe the nerve of that guy?" Ruth huffed as they left the courtroom. "Puts me through all this and then doesn't have the balls to go through with it."

"You know what I can't believe?" Zoey hissed right back. "That you are looking this gift horse in the mouth. A half hour ago you were looking at a fine, or a jail sentence. Don't forget that."

"Who in their right mind shows up to a felony hearing without an attorney?"

Zoey and Ruth turned in unison to the direction of the sound. Blake was already making his way toward them. Had he been in the courtroom the whole time, or had he just arrived? He looked positively handsome in his navy suit, gold-cuff-link-wearing, clean-shaven sort of way. Zoey had already seen this side of him, something that Ruth refused to acknowledge. He also looked uncharacteristically mad as hell, something Ruth may have been more familiar with.

"Why on earth didn't you bring a lawyer?" Blake repeated when he caught up with them.

"Because we both already know who was holding all the cards. Why would I throw money away when it was clear judge clown shoes wanted to make sure I suffered? I might've needed that cash to buy cigarettes," Ruth replied.

"You don't smoke," Blake said.

"No, but I wanted to have them to trade and buy myself out of work detail. Or getting beat up."

Blake's face showed no signs of appreciating her joke.

"Relax," Ruth went on, giving Blake a playful tug on his sleeve. "I did my own research. I was pretty sure a jackass like him wouldn't take it all the way, so I just went in and played dumb. If he did show up today, the judge would probably call a continuance and insist that I get a lawyer. So, you see, it all worked out. Now, come on, let's hit the nearest pub. I'm buying."

Blake didn't move, even as Ruth started walking toward the exit doors.

"Do you want to know why Randy Hollister didn't show up today?" Blake said.

Ruth halted, turning back around. "I just told you why."

"And maybe you are right," Blake replied. "Maybe he didn't show up because it wasn't worth the trouble. But maybe it's possible he called it all off because I threatened him."

"You did what?" Zoey and Ruth said in unison.

Blake showed the smallest hint of a smile. "Let's say I appealed to his practical side. I told him that if he thought you made a scene at the bar, imagine what you could do on a witness stand. If nothing else, you would turn him into a laughingstock. And I warned him that I would do everything in my power to see you represented by the kind of publicity-hungry attorney who would find and publicly parade every girl he hit on that night. I told him that if he continued with this pride-fueled vendetta, by the time this was over, he would likely lose not only his wife, but also his job. Maybe even get disbarred."

"How did you even know about this?" Ruth said, trying to mask her surprise.

"I was at the party, remember?" Blake said in exasperation.

"Told you," Zoey said.

"I don't recall asking for your help." Ruth huffed.

They engaged in a brief stare down, Blake looking disenchanted and Ruth, indignant.

"Thanks, Blake," Zoey finally said to try and break the tension. "You're a lifesaver."

Ruth rounded on Zoey. "Don't speak for me. I didn't ask for anyone's assistance."

"Enough." Blake's voice stopped Ruth in her tracks.

Ruth and Zoey both looked at Blake, who was shaking his head and running a hand through his neatly combed hair.

"I can't do this anymore," he said, once he was sure he had Ruth's attention. "I don't want to."

Blake no longer looked angry. He looked deflated. He was always brooding, but now his whole posture held the weight of a sadness that was near to breaking Zoey's heart.

Ruth must have noticed it too, because she was back to trying to sound airy and carefree.

"Look, I'm sorry." She laughed cheerfully. "Thanks for coming to the rescue. I'm grateful. Now don't be mad at me, okay? I've had a rough day."

Blake's face didn't change. In fact, his frown got deeper. Zoey thought he was going to turn and walk away but instead he said, near to a whisper, "I wanted you to need me."

"What kind of bullshit is that?" Ruth replied crossly.

"I wanted us to need each other. Ruth, I've been waiting almost a year to catch you in between hookups and drama. So that maybe I could convince you to give a relationship with me a try. I've had feelings for you since the first time I saw you. I've replayed the night we spent together in my mind a thousand times. After my marriage broke up, I never thought I'd feel that way about another woman again. I'm sorry if I stuck my nose in where it didn't belong. I waited for days after your arrest for you to tell me about it. It hurt so much that you didn't, but I thought that maybe you were too embarrassed. Now I realize, you'll never need me. I don't think you'll ever need anybody. But I don't want to be your secret bodyguard anymore. And I can't be your friend. I'm sorry, Ruth, but the party's over for me."

His voice had started to tremble by the end. He was crushed—it was written all over his face. Any fool could see. Zoey wished the floor would open up and swallow her, to remove her from being privy to this painful conversation.

Blake didn't wait for a response. As soon as he finished, he turned on his heel and walked away. Zoey looked to Ruth, waiting for her sister to follow him and not let him get away. But Ruth was watching Blake leave too, her arms crossed over her chest and her mouth slightly agape.

"What the hell is wrong with you?" Zoey said accusingly, breaking Ruth out of her reverie.

"What? Don't look at me like that. I had no idea he felt that way."

"Well, now you know."

"I'll call him later, it'll be fine." Ruth tried to resume her breezy tone.

"You think a man like Blake makes that sort of speech just to hear himself talk?" Zoey spat, shaking her head in pure disgust. "You're an idiot."

Zoey thought she might actually start to scream. Not only had Ruth come out on top in another one of her escapades, but another man also had been kicked to the curb after having jumped through enormous hoops to get her attention. Only this was a good man, who didn't deserve a casual blow-off. With a snort of derision, Zoey followed Blake out the door, ignoring the single time Ruth called her name. Ruth was on her own with this one, Zoey reflected.

Back out on the street, Zoey blinked at the sun, which temporarily blinded her, then headed in the direction of home. *Everything always works out for Ruth*, Zoey once again marveled. The only lesson Ruth had learned was that she really did have the power to make men act like morons. Shaking her head and muttering to herself, Zoey turned into the first liquor store she saw.

When Tristan opened the door, Zoey was already light-headed and leaning against the wall beside it.

"I'm seeking refuge," she said.

"This can't be good," he murmured as she sauntered past him into the living room, carrying a brown paper bag with a bottle in it.

"It went badly for Ruth?" Tristan asked when he joined her.

"Oh no," Zoey said dramatically, taking another swallow out of the bottle after landing on the couch. "It went just dandy. All the charges were dropped and she got off without so much as a warning."

"Then why have you taken to getting drunk in public?"

"Who says I'm drunk?" Zoey countered.

"What you're doing right here is what I like to call 'Classic American Wino.'"

Zoey held up the bottle by the top of the neck and let the bag slip off and fall to the ground, revealing a single bottle of Mike's Hard Lemonade. "For your information, this isn't wine, it's a malt beverage. Unfortunately, they wouldn't sell me a single bottle, so I took it upon myself to distribute the rest of the pack to some legit winos, but they didn't care about hiding them. So there."

"I stand corrected."

"I would also like to point out that the whole notion that your weight is somehow relevant to how much liquor you can hold is a bunch of tripe," Zoey added after draining what was left in the bottle. "Another one of these and I'd be seeing double."

"Have you eaten?"

"No." She snorted. "I was busy getting the Teflon Dominatrix ready for court."

Tristan laughed a little and sat down on the couch beside her. "I'm not sure I understand what the problem is. It sounds like a positive outcome, so why is your nose so out of joint?"

"Because this has been happening for the better part of my life! For as long as I can remember, Ruth has been doing irresponsible stuff and someone, usually me, is always covering for her or picking up the pieces. I'm sick of her always getting exactly what she wants. I'm sick of her not caring if she hurts people."

Zoey stopped, midrant. There was so much more she wanted to vent. How Zoey had become sick to death of catering to Ruth's need for immediate gratification. Zoey wanted to rage and then weep with the realization that she had jumped from the frying pan into the fire when she married Derek, who had many of the same characteristics.

She looked over at Tristan, who hadn't even attempted to get a word in edgewise. He was merely listening, with the occasional nod of his head.

"Ruth fought for her right to party and she's been

partying ever since." Zoey sighed wearily. "I'm tired of always having to be the grown-up."

"I hear you. It sounds infuriating. As someone who doesn't have any siblings, I can't really relate. But maybe because she knows she can count on you to catch her if she falls, she feels free to take bigger risks?"

He was calm and levelheaded as always, refusing to see anything but the good side of people. Through the buzz of hard lemonade and the fog of anger, Tristan still managed to soothe her.

"I think you've been under a great deal of stress. It's completely understandable."

He put a gentle hand on her knee. A friendly gesture that managed to send her already scattered nerves reeling. With an impulse brought on by dizziness and a myriad of emotions, she reached over and wrapped both arms around his neck.

He didn't return the hug, didn't rub her back and coo to her that everything was going to be all right. He stiffened, his arms awkwardly at his sides until she pulled back and placed her lips against his smooth cheek.

"Thanks, Tristan," she whispered in his ear after the kiss. "You're a sanity saver for sure."

He clumsily gave her back several pats. Zoey felt the hesitation and pulled away from him, took note of the discomfort written on his face, and flushed with guilt and embarrassment. Being attracted to him was a mistake. Touching him was a bigger one. She hadn't shown up at his door looking for commiseration, she was looking for him to save her. The thought triggered a surge of renewed anger. The only thing she could do was fall back on her old standby of making a hasty retreat.

"I have to go," Zoey said abruptly, standing up.

Tristan stood up too. "Zoey, wait. Don't leave. You're tipsy. I'll make you something to eat."

"I'm fine," she said quickly, handing her empty bottle to him. "Can you throw this out for me?"

"At least let me call—" he began.

"Don't you dare say it!" She cut him off with a talk-to-the-hand motion in his direction. "I don't need your car service. I don't need your food. I don't need your attempts at chivalry. I know how to both walk and hail a cab. I'm sorry I bothered you with this."

The last thing she saw was his dumbfounded look when she turned back around at the door.

"This isn't your fault. I just have to get back to doing what's best for me."

He nodded silently, with bewildered eyes, as the door closed behind her.

Chapter 16

When it came to Tristan Malloy, it was time for Zoey to start implementing some self-control. The crush had gotten too big. She wasn't going to be able to wean herself off him; she was going to have to go cold turkey. Armed with Ruth's original and knowledgeable advice, Zoey went about the business of keeping her distance from Tristan. She was prepared to deploy all the polite ways to avoid him, but she couldn't shake the rush when she so much as thought about him. For the first day, every time her phone chimed, she was filled with dread that it was Tristan, followed by disappointment when it wasn't. She had gotten used to hearing from him daily. The way she had stormed out of his place had likely freaked him out. She tried to look at that as a positive thing.

Ruth didn't return to their apartment until the morning after her court date. She walked in as if nothing unusual had happened the day before. In fact, she looked like she was basking in afterglow.

"You're in an awfully good mood," Zoey said begrudgingly.

"It is a beautiful day," Ruth replied, still looking dreamy.

"Guess you found a replacement for Blake?" Zoey couldn't help delivering the jab. Did Ruth understand the consequences of taking someone for granted?

"As a matter of fact, I did." Ruth was beaming. "I like to call him Blake 2.0, the reboot."

"I don't get it."

"After I was so rudely abandoned at the courthouse, I did some thinking. You were right, I had turned Blake into Mr. Dependable. I didn't appreciate him. I texted and called him about a hundred times until he finally answered. I insisted that I was coming over to his apartment. I apologized profusely, then sat like a good girl while he vented his spleen. His ranting had nothing to do with me. There was a lot about this wedding coming up that the bachelor party at the Marquee was for. About how his ex-wife was going to be at the wedding with her new boyfriend. How disgustingly sweet they were. Now Hollister would be shooting daggers at him through the whole affair as well. I waited until I was sure he was almost done, then I kissed him. Mostly to shut him up. Then I told him I would go with him to the wedding as the most refined dame he ever saw. Then we had the most impolite night in recent memory."

"Who doesn't love a happy ending?" Zoey's voice was half awe, half sarcasm.

"He's so proper. I thought he was too buttoned up. But this time?" Ruth gushed, accompanied by a long languid stretch. "A complete freak between the sheets!"

Considering just how many freaks Ruth had kept company with over the years, that was quite an endorsement. Zoey prayed she wouldn't offer details. She didn't want her impression of Blake tainted with images of him wearing a leather full-head mask with a zipper for a mouth or trussing Ruth up like a turkey. But there was something else. Ruth's voice changed when she spoke about Blake. She sounded . . . respectful. And sweet, even. When Ruth packed a small bag before leaving for work and told Zoey she was spending the night at Blake's, Zoey knew it was serious. Blake was getting two nights in a row, during the week, no less. That was unprecedented.

All Zoey knew was that she was going to be left alone, which she thought was a blessing. She needed time to figure out her own next move, starting with pushing her life's reset button, even if that meant ghosting Tristan Malloy. She couldn't bring herself to delete his phone number, but she would forget it existed. One day turned into two, then to three. Zoey's spirits started to sag on day four and she waged an internal battle with the urge to text Tristan a quick hello. What if he had overdosed on late-night television or was shaking in a cold sweat after binge-watching *The Walking Dead*? But she couldn't run that risk. If that hello led to an invitation, she would be tempted to accept. She had to stop the cycle for his sake as well as hers. She spent days four and five questioning why she would take love life advice from her freewheeling heartbreaker of a sister to begin with. Ruth, who had resurfaced while Blake went out of town for business, resumed making herself scarce after Zoey nearly bit her head off after a casual question or two.

By day six of the cold turkey, she conceded all hope was lost. He had never gone that long without making some sort of contact. Adding insult to injury, she hadn't received a single call for a job booking. She spent the whole day systematically eating everything she could get her hands on, emptying both the fridge and the pantry.

On day seven, she was downright pissed off. A stupid kiss on the cheek and a hug scared him off? She hadn't groped or propositioned him. She hadn't thrown herself at him. Why would she want to be with someone so timid and skittish anyway? The anger lingered through the weekend despite numerous invitations from her sister to get out of the apartment. She spent that Sunday snarling on the couch, with Ruth shooting her sideways glances of genuine concern. She ordered takeout all day, at one point tipping the delivery person a handful of dimes, nickels, and pennies because she'd run out of money. Not completely out of money, but she would need her quarters if she was ever going to wash clothes again.

Zoey started that Monday with an attitude adjustment. A new week called for a new perspective. A pity party was fine but turning it into a vacation was not. Tristan Malloy hadn't asked for her help; she had offered it. Having an extended temper tantrum because things didn't work out as planned was not only childish, but also plain old stupid. She was the one who deviated from her original strategy of taking this year to work on herself. It was time to get back to it. She promised herself, starting today, she was going to dig in. Her sole focus was to start drumming up some business. She would place new ads, call on previous clients to say hi and tell them all the new things she was working on. She would test new recipes. Zoey checked her bank account on her phone and sighed. She refused to dip into the nest egg she had put away. She had drawn up a budget, and she was sticking to it. How many ways could she dress up Kraft mac and cheese?

Then a text came through. A text from Tristan Malloy.

MORNING! CAN YOU WORK FOR ME WEDNESDAY NIGHT?

She shook her head in disbelief. What the hell? She had just released him into the universe an hour ago. Now he was back. And worse, he reentered with the only offer she couldn't refuse. With hands that needed steadying she texted back.

SURE
GREAT! I'LL HAVE EVERYTHING YOU NEED HERE. ARRIVE AT FIVE. THINK FRENCH.

There was no further conversation. No playful banter. No sharing any new tidbits of discovery on his part. Tristan didn't even let her suggest the menu. Her heart wouldn't stop fluttering, even as she reminded herself that it really was time to let him go. They could still be friends, a conclusion that left her feeling successful and at the same time forlorn. But, if nothing else, she was able to redirect her focus back on what she had set out to accomplish. The clock was nearly out of time before she was getting back her name and going out all on her own. Nothing and nobody was going to get in her way.

Chapter 17

Whaen he opened the door to let her in, he still looked so good. This time, however, Tristan's nervousness echoed the night she met him. All the gaming equipment was gone from the living room. He made no mention of the way she had stormed out the last time they were together, which was depressing in its own right. Once she followed him into the kitchen, she found out why.

"I have a favor to ask of you," Tristan said. "A big one."

"Okay," Zoey said warily as she scanned the very simple menu and the recipe for the main course he had placed on the center island. There was something foreboding; this was a dinner for two.

"I only have one guest coming tonight." Tristan rushed through the words as he watched her read through the directions. "A woman. A date. I have a date."

"Oh." Zoey managed to get the one word past the tightening in her chest. Suddenly, trying to tell the joke about not poisoning anyone didn't seem so funny. She managed to plaster on a smile. "That's great. You really came out of your shell. I could've delivered a pep talk over the phone."

"That's not the favor though. I want you to stay in here." He began to trip over his words. "I don't want her to know you're here."

Anger began to mix in with the heartbreak. "Tristan, you know how to cook. You don't need me."

"But I do. I really do."

"Then let me get to work and I'll leave as soon as I'm done."

"This isn't about the food, Zoey. Do you remember Kristin, from the night we met?"

"Hard to forget the only other woman in the room." Zoey sighed. A good veal and cream sauce was going to go to waste being fed to that little slip of a thing. She could picture the plate coming back into the kitchen with all the vegetables being picked out and the rest of it going into the trash. Tristan was too preoccupied to catch her frown.

"I got up the nerve to call her and ask her out for dinner last week."

He had taken Kristin out on a date. Zoey had been eating her weight in comfort food for over a week while he was out having fun. She had done so well on her little makeover project, and the final outcome was like a sudden and unexpected punch to the gut. At least there was one saving grace: she had never made her true feelings known. She had managed to save face, even if she was going to spend the next week in bed, crying until there were no tears left.

"It was a horror show. She's educated and knows a lot about a lot of things. But conversation kept reverting back to politics and current events, stuff I don't feel comfortable with."

"Nobody should bring up politics on a date." Zoey's face scrunched up in what she hoped looked like aversion, while she was secretly pleased as punch at his misstep. "Talk about a mood killer."

"I thought that maybe you could stay in here and if I get stumped on something, I can rush in here and ask you."

"I don't know diddly about politics other than it can turn any family dinner into a brawl."

"You've got to know more than I do."

He did have a point there. Zoey stuck the tip of her

pointer finger into her mouth and began to chew at her cuticle. She forced her hand back to her side before she drew blood.

"This sounds like a backward *Cyrano de Bergerac*."

That solicited a smile from Tristan. "It does, doesn't it? Only there's no love triangle going on."

Yes, there was. He just didn't realize it.

"Can't you segue the conversation to art and literature? Things you know about?"

"I tried. But she's an activity person, likes the outdoors."

"What about golf?"

"She plays tennis. And it looks like golf is a sticking point for her to boot. All the guys at work play and she's never invited."

"Music?" The vision of him as his Aerosmith alter ego flashed before her eyes. She cursed herself.

"That's a good one! I'll use it tonight." He brightened, which hurt her case more than helped it. "See? This is what I'm talking about. You can throw me lifelines when I need them. I felt so lost on our last date, I almost had a panic attack in the middle of dinner."

Zoey wondered if he knew he was pulling at her heartstrings. Then she wondered if he kissed Kristin good night.

"I can't begin to list all the ways this is a bad idea. You should start a relationship as the real you. It's more than enough, trust me."

He spoke like he hadn't heard her. "Please, Zoey? You can name your price to stay. And if you hadn't told me to not watch the news, I'd at least know some of the things she's talking about."

She didn't think he had it in him to play the blame card. To remind Zoey that she was partially responsible for the mess.

"By the way, I did start watching the news this week. You're right. It's depressing as hell," Tristan added. "But I don't think it's going to be enough. You're my rock, Zoey. I need you here."

Zoey tried one last time. "Okay, that's fine. But hiding me is dishonest."

"Not if she doesn't know you're here and I don't bring it up."

Zoey shook her head at her own disgrace. She had successfully turned a wonderful upstanding spirit into every other self-serving human on the planet. If his next sentence turned out to be "You owe me" she might start to cry. There would be plenty of time for tears. But right now, she needed some income, and that meant swallowing her pride.

"This is the first and last time I'm going to do this," she relented.

"I just need to get one successful date under my belt." Tristan's optimism returned with his relief. He was oblivious to her turmoil. "If I can get through one date without breaking out into a cold sweat or passing out, I'll be golden. Thanks, Zoey, you're a good friend."

"You're welcome." She tried to keep the disappointment out of her voice. "Now please step away from the fridge, so I can get started."

He didn't notice her curtness. She couldn't help noticing he had already done most of the prep for the meal. She'd be spending most of her time watching pots boil and skulking behind the doors whenever they opened. She drew the line at sitting on the floor behind the island or pushing herself up against the wall. Zoey put on one of his aprons and went to work while Tristan paced the apartment. She tried to keep her head down and focus, but she would look up every time he made a lap by her, leaving the familiar trail of Old Spice in his wake. It was the only thing she recognized in the man she'd originally met.

"Why don't you go put on some music?" Zoey suggested, mainly to give herself something to listen to other than the voices in her head telling her all the ways she could ruin his evening. Dangerous thoughts to have when handling raw meat. Or holding a knife.

"Excellent idea." He bolted out of the kitchen. A minute later, chamber music started playing through the speakers above her. Classy. She sliced an onion she didn't need in half and began to chop it, looking forward to the watery eyes it might produce.

"How do I look?" he asked when he came back into the kitchen, checking the clock again.

Gorgeous, she thought, checking out the new power suit he was wearing. Something he had bought himself. He had also gotten a haircut, shorter on the sides and longer on top with a healthy waving that flipped to the side. It looked smashing. He no longer needed her, which she should be viewing as a blessing. After this was over, he was on his own. She meant it this time. She had to stop being a glutton for punishment. It only added to the heartbreak.

"Perfect," she said. It was gruffer than she intended.

"Any last-minute advice?" Tristan asked.

There were so many things she wanted to tell him. At the top of that list was screaming "Pick me! Can't you see how I feel about you?" The next would be to tell him that this whole affair was doomed to fail, which should've brought her more joy. Guilt always made for a good motivator. She stopped working and studied him.

"People's favorite topic is usually themselves. If you feel yourself slipping, just encourage her to talk about what interests her. It'll keep the conversation flowing. And don't worry about not knowing what she's talking about, just ask her to explain, only look fascinated when you do it. I've been with people who I didn't get a word in edgewise with all night. If you're a good listener, it has the added bonus of learning a lot about a person."

"Keep her talking about herself," Tristan repeated. "Got it."

All conversation stopped when the doorbell rang.

"It's showtime." He stole her phrase while pulling at his jacket and double-checking his tie.

"Good luck," she told him. After he left she added, "I think you're going to need it."

Zoey moved about the kitchen as quietly as she could and decided that no matter how this scheme played out, this was the last time she was going to see Tristan Malloy. She had the best of intentions and made her mistakes, but she no longer had the strength or desire to watch him find his happily ever after. Even sadder, if the evening played out the way he wanted it to, he wouldn't miss her. He'd be on his way to new adventures.

As soon as she was done putting the finishing touches on the salads, he came through the door adjacent to the dining room to retrieve them.

"Things are going great," he whispered, way too close to her ear, his breath tickling the back of her neck. "Your advice was stellar."

He grabbed the salad plates and left before she could respond, careful to not let the door swing open too wide.

He didn't want soup, and she knew why. It's a course that could get sloppy. Zoey sulked. There would be no napkin bibs making an appearance this evening. It was becoming more and more apparent that he wanted her there only for moral support. An interesting turn of phrase, since morals obviously weren't on tonight's menu.

Tristan snuck back through the door with the empty salad plates a half hour later.

"We have a few seconds." He still was whispering. "She went to the ladies' room."

Zoey hastily started to plate the main course. "Then here, let's get this on the table and you can meet her in the living room when she comes out."

"It's going so well." Tristan beamed while reaching into his pocket and pulling out several one-hundred-dollar bills. "I can't thank you enough. Being in my own space makes it so much easier."

"Home field advantage, right?" she muttered, reaching for the money he held out to her.

"Listen, I think I can handle dessert on my own," he said, and Zoey felt like she had fallen on her own knife.

"As soon as you two are back in the dining room, I'll just slip out the door." All pretense of them being in some grand conspiracy together had vanished. She had been paid for services she hadn't rendered and that was fine by Zoey. He could clean up his kitchen on his own. She just had to hold it together for a few more minutes and she would be free of this whole surreptitious affair. And him.

She garnished the plates with parsley and he dashed out to the dining room.

"Just wanted to see if I could lend a hand."

Zoey whirled around and was face-to-face with Kristin, who had decided to take a detour back from the bathroom through the kitchen. Kristin's expression was one of mild surprise. When Tristan burst through the door to the kitchen, his was more akin to horror. Zoey, in the middle, looked from one to the other, feeling the heat rush of embarrassment.

"Kristin!" Tristan exclaimed, cemented where he stood. "I'd like to introduce you to Zoey."

Zoey turned back to Kristin with a feeble "Hi."

Kristin approached Zoey, extending a delicate hand. "It's nice to meet you, Zoey. I can see you have everything under control in here."

"I was just finishing up. And getting ready to leave." Zoey tried to sound light and breezy as she shook Kristin's hand with her now-clammy one. "Nice to meet you too."

"Well then, don't let me get in your way. Dinner smells delicious. Tristan, I'll wait for you in the dining room." Kristin passed by both of them, and through the dining room door.

Zoey took a quick look at Tristan, and they exchanged panic-stricken wordless shrugs before he took off after Kristin.

The proper thing for Zoey to do would be to leave. This was not her problem. Her prediction had come to fruition. It served Tristan right to have this thing explode on its own accord.

Zoey tiptoed over to the dining room door and tentatively placed her ear to the tiny crack available. The only sounds she could make out were muffled voices in quiet conversation. She held her breath to try and get a better listen when the voices became more hushed. She did everything short of pushing at the door to get a better view. Being busted twice in one day was more than she thought she could handle.

"That did not go well," he said from behind her. Zoey instantly straightened back up, caught red-handed when he came back into the kitchen through the other door. Busted anyway. At this point, what did it matter?

"I would say not." No point in mincing words either.

"Kristin called it a night. I should've listened to you. Turns out hiding a woman in your kitchen looks sketchy to the one in the dining room," he said with a smirk. It was odd, given the gravity of the statement.

"Who knew? Oh yeah, I did." Gloating was wrong, especially when secretly elated. He didn't appear too devastated. "You don't look too worse for wear."

"It wasn't a total loss. She left me with some insight."

"Is that the reason for the grin?"

"Very astute. Kristin prides herself on being astute too. She remembered you from the first time she was here. She said when she caught us, we had the kind of guilt on our faces that was disproportionate to the situation. She told me we should never play poker with anyone but each other."

"That's probably solid advice too. I'm guessing your love connection was just cut off at the knees?"

"Turns out we both had ulterior motives. It's not that you were here that she took issue with, it was the plot to keep you out of sight. According to Kristin, I did this to get your attention, maybe make you jealous. She wasn't all that hurt. She thought I was attractive enough to go along with dating me. If she managed to get me to take the offer her company tendered, it would be a real coup. And she'd get a chance to upstage her obnoxious boss. She is hardly heartbroken. I kept telling her that you and I were just friends, but she wasn't convinced. And I think she may be right. Once again, I did it all wrong. I really am a hopeless case. I'm so sorry I made you a part of this. You're a much better friend than I deserve. Now if you'll excuse me, I'm going to go drown in a bottle of chardonnay before I embarrass you, or myself, any further."

Tristan left the kitchen before Zoey could think of the right words to say. That Kristin was only partially correct. All three of them had ulterior motives, but currently, only two of them had come clean. Zoey didn't want to leave any room for any further misunderstandings when it came to Tristan. She started to untie, then took off her apron.

Chapter 18

Zoey was waiting for Tristan when he came back into the kitchen. He didn't appear drunk and wasn't holding any wine bottles, but he had removed his jacket and tie. The first two buttons of his shirt were undone. If she wasn't so nervous, she may have gotten a better laugh out of his initial look after he stopped short. It was one of complete and utter astonishment.

"I wanted to make sure you were all right," she said casually, watching him struggle to keep eye contact. Then she giggled.

"Did you?" he replied with widening eyes that were incapable of tearing themselves away from her. "At this moment, I have to confess, I don't know what I am."

Zoey had been busy while he was indisposed. A no-holds-barred, last-ditch effort to force his hand into admitting how he felt or telling her once and for all that he felt nothing. She had stripped down to bare skin, and the only thing standing between him and the full monty was the strategically placed apron she had put back on. She leaned against the counter, the granite making contact on her bare back like ice on her hot skin, and cocked a hip, generating a provocative sway in the apron's skirt.

"How about aroused?" Zoey made an exaggerated move to double-check that the apron bib top was covering her nipples by sensually running her hands along the sides of her breasts to underneath them. Then she gave them a slight push up. She peered up at him with feigned innocence from beneath long lashes. "Aroused would be good."

"That works." Tristan breathed, his gaze following the slow movement of her hands.

He had gotten bolder with taking her all in. His eyes alone were generating heat. She brazenly let her gaze settle on the zipper of his pants. Nope, not quite excited enough. She slowly turned around and looked back over her shoulder.

His eyes were riveted on her round, full, bare bottom.

"How about now?" she asked, giving her booty a shake.

His pants and what was in them finally got with the program and gave the proper response. The look on his face left her wondering if she may have done too much too soon and he was going to take her right there, bent over the kitchen counter.

"I've never been good at taking a hint." He mustered the strength to look up and meet her gaze. "But this one is hard to miss."

She turned her head around to the wall again and ever so slowly pulled at the bow tied at the small of her back until she felt it give way. Then she turned to face him, aware that the now-untethered apron was rewarding him with another quick glimpse, this time from the front.

"I thought it was time that I stopped being stupid and told you how I really felt about you, but I was having trouble finding the right words."

"Message received," Tristan said, his hands moving to the front of his shirt.

It was right about then that the tide turned and Zoey began to lose her advantage. A moment ago, his eyes were smiling. Now there was nothing but smolder.

"I like my guests to feel comfortable," he said, his hands moving to his shirt. He began to work the third button, which was still fastened.

"Well, you were raised in the hospitality business,"

she teased, her eyes now glued to his hands moving on to the next button down.

"One of us here is completely overdressed," he said, and another button was released.

"Guess we better fix that." She jokingly made like she was going to remove the apron but only pulled the skirt of it up to her thighs. She heard his sudden intake of air and then let it drop to her knees again. None of it stopped him from his task, but he did skip the last button and pulled the shirt over his head, taking his undershirt with it. She could only stare at his chiseled upper body and give a quick prayer of thanks that breathing was an involuntary act.

"You are a very naughty girl." He had gotten comfortable, playful. He had been worth the wait. "Not to mention you could catch your death of cold and I wish I was in my leather pants."

"I thought we were taking clothes off, not putting them on." Her voice took on a throaty tone. He began taking steps to close the distance between them.

When he reached her, he watched his own hand brush his knuckles along the side of her breast. She heard her own gasp, when his hand went under the apron to cup her full breast, his thumb toying with the now-tight little bud in the center. He gave her nipple a slight pinch and Zoey leaned back against the counter, her hands grabbing onto the sinewy arms when she felt the blood rush to her head.

"I hope this isn't the only time we do this." His lips were getting closer, already starting to pucker. "Every fantasy I had about you included taking your clothes off."

He pressed his lips to hers while his free hand moved to her other breast. He cared. Had fantasized about her. All the needlessly wasted time to make up for. She wrapped her arms around his neck and opened her mouth to let her tongue brush along his bottom lip. It was all the encouragement he needed to plunder her mouth, and his tongue delved inside to steal what was left of her breath away. His hard sex pressed through his now-inconvenient pants and against her. She shifted to grind against him, starting to shake with need. His hand traveled lower beneath the apron, over her rib cage, and down her hip. His hand splayed across her stomach and then went lower. He started her wiggling when a thick nimble finger slipped inside her. She arched her back and tore her mouth from his to gasp for air when a second finger joined in the gentle massaging that set all her nerve endings to pulsate.

"Zoey, please tell me this isn't some kind of joke." He groaned as his lips grazed past her ear on into her neck and his fingers returned to her hip, freeing her from his exquisite torture. "Please tell me this isn't my punishment for what I made you do tonight."

She held his head in her hands, and they both stilled.

"I don't want to punish you and I don't want to tease you. I want to feel you. All of you. Inside me."

Without another word, he took her hand and they raced down the hallway to his bedroom.

"I would carry you," he said halfway to their final destination, "but I feel weak in the knees."

"Then we're even. In every fantasy I've had about you, you picked me up and whisked me away."

"Next time," he said, stopping short and pulling her to him then kissing her hard.

Upon reaching the bedroom, he released the clip that held her hair back, then pulled at the last remaining apron tie. Zoey rushed to unzipper his pants while they were still in motion to reach the bed. Tristan impatiently kicked off his remaining clothing and tumbled them both back onto the crisp, clean comforter. She longed to touch every part of him.

His lack of experience was easily made up for by his hunger. He took his time worshipping every inch of her. She could feel him smiling up against all her most sensitive spots as he kissed them, the back of her neck, along her rib cage, and behind her knees. She was soon engulfed in all-encompassing lust. Zoey wanted them to take their time, make the connection meaningful for both of them. But she was losing that battle, touch by skin-scorching touch. His kiss returned to her lips and she felt his hardness, inches away from her throbbing core.

"Condom," she murmured into his neck as her fingernails raked lightly down his back.

"Right," he growled while pushing himself off the bed. "Right, right right."

"Please tell me you have one." She sighed, missing his touch already.

"I don't only have one," he said while sprinting to the bathroom, his backside a glorious feast for her heavily lidded eyes. "I have a box of them."

"Check the expiration date!" Zoey called after him.

"They're good," he replied, rushing to jump back on the bed. "I celebrate New Year's with a fresh box."

If Zoey had her way, he'd be needing a new box by the end of the week, not December.

Together they fumbled and giggled their way through putting the condom on. He shivered with her touch and he hissed through clenched teeth as she rolled the latex to his hilt and ended the exercise with a nip at his belly.

"I can't hold back much longer," he ground out.

"I don't want you to." She panted as he pushed her down onto the bed, and kissed her all the way back to the pillows, where her head came to rest.

She opened herself to him and he thrust himself deep inside her. Both their worlds went still. Tristan hovered over her, staring down at her intently.

"Am I doing something wrong?" Zoey asked, grabbing onto his arms and wriggling beneath him.

"I want to remember you like this forever."

There wasn't a single part of her that didn't feel the impact of the heartfelt wonderment written on his face. The affection in his voice, the passion in his eyes. She could already feel herself starting to tingle, in the deepest recesses of her soul.

Then she wrapped a leg around him and smiled.

It was all the encouragement he needed. They began a different kind of dance. The kind that left her reeling.

Chapter 19

Several condoms and a surprisingly refreshing sleep later, Zoey was awakened to the scent of coffee. Her eyes fluttered open, adjusted to the daylight, and found Tristan sitting on the bed beside her, a steaming mug in his hand. He had showered and thrown on a pair of shorts but nothing else. He was as sexy in the light of day as he was the night before.

"Did I overstay my welcome?" she asked, snuggling under the covers, and the coffee smell mixed with the intoxicating scent of him on her pillow. She ran her tongue over her teeth and resisted the urge to dash off to his bathroom to brush her teeth with toothpaste and her finger.

"Not at all," he replied, taking a sip out of the mug. "I was taking a minute to enjoy watching you sleep."

If anyone else had said that to her, it might've sounded creepy. But Tristan was just basking in the same afterglow she was also feeling. Never before had Zoey been treated to lovemaking that was completely about her. Her comfort, her desire, her pleasure. All his enjoyment was derived from watching and taking part in hers. It took intimacy to a whole new level. Her orgasms were shattering and he was left shuddering for minutes after his. The memory alone was enough to set her skin ablaze all over again. For him, it was new and amazing, and she found herself getting caught up in it. She wanted him to feel appreciated too. It wasn't just sex with Tristan. It was lovemaking, in every sense of the word. She couldn't remember the last time it all felt so real.

"When I woke up and saw you next to me I couldn't believe it. Part of me thought it was a dream."

"I must look a wreck," she said, sitting up and running a hand through her tousled hair. Muscles that had long gone unused voiced protest. She gingerly wrapped the sheets halfway around her. It wasn't something she did out of modesty, but she knew that tone of his voice. A thorough sexing was sure to follow. He may have time he wanted to make up for, but she needed to try and ensure that they rested for a while. She needed to build up some stamina. She eyed his coffee, and without saying a word, Tristan held out his mug.

Zoey wrapped both hands around the cup and blew at the hot brew within it. Tristan reached out and tucked a wayward lock of her hair behind her ear. Then he brushed his hand across her cheek and cupped her face, tilting her head up to meet his gaze.

"You are so beautiful," he told her tenderly, each word perfectly enunciated, "in every way."

He sounded sincere, which only served to embarrass her. False flattery she could handle. There was nothing false about Tristan.

"I think you need this more than I do." She thrust the coffee back in his direction, trying to laugh the statement off.

"Not before you have some." He smiled, then looked serious. "Unless you want a cup of your own?"

"Now we're going to worry about swapping germs? I think that ship has sailed." Zoey giggled and brought the cup to her mouth. She peered at him from above the rim and marveled. He liked his coffee the exact same way she did, not too light, not too sweet.

"Any regrets this morning?" Tristan asked, again in all seriousness.

"Just that I wish I hadn't ditched my yoga when I moved up here," she responded, blushing. "You?"

"One big one. All the time I wasted fighting how I felt about you. It's probably time I come clean about Kristin as well. I only asked her out to try and get you out of my head."

"And if I didn't feel so honor bound to get through this year before insisting on my divorce, I would've made my feelings known a lot sooner too."

Silence lingered. She had just introduced the elephant in the room. But pretending Derek didn't exist wasn't going to make him go away. The timing, however, after their first night together, was awful. Zoey was new at this too.

"Regret is a wasted emotion." She handed the coffee back to him, followed by winding her hand around his neck and pulling him in for a long, lingering kiss. Her morning rituals could wait. He had already made her take leave of all her senses, and she was more than willing to throw morning mouth slime onto the pile. His breath was sweet and fresh and she couldn't care less. His fingertips traced up along her spine and weaved into her hair. He shifted and pulled her closer to him. His kiss deepened, had turned greedy in the need to plunder her mouth. Screw resting and stamina building. Whenever his lips touched hers, it triggered her want for more of him. All of him.

Suddenly, to her dismay, he pulled away.

"Hold tight," he said, reaching for the phone. "I have to cancel my tee time."

Her smile grew wide. He wanted to cancel playing golf to play with her. Maybe she had two regrets, starting something she herself wasn't sure she felt up to finishing.

"Don't cancel," she said, halting him in middial. She wanted to see him doing what he loved. She wanted to send the clear message that if it was something that was important to him, then it was important to her too. It wasn't all about her, no matter how much he was willing to prove otherwise. Zoey wanted to give back.

"I don't want to leave you," Tristan protested.

"I second that! I want to come with you."

"You want to play golf with me?"

"Well, I don't know about playing . . . but I'd be more than willing to try and learn." *More like watch you*, a correction she kept to herself. And see what the maximum speed of a golf cart was.

He looked so genuinely excited, her eyes began to glisten.

"I would love that," he said.

"Sure, you say that now. Let's see how you feel when eighteen holes takes eighteen hours."

"I have all the time in the world." He winked at her

and gave her knee a squeeze. "I'll let you shower. We leave in thirty minutes."

Their car called to take them to the golf course but had to wait an extra fifteen minutes when Zoey became infatuated with Tristan's shower. It was nothing like the shower in Ruth's apartment. For the last eleven months, she had stood under the calcium-coated two-output showerhead that spit water of various temperatures ranging from icy to scalding. Zoey hadn't given it much thought until she experienced the luxuriousness that was this shower. Not only was it as big as some apartments, but it also had a giant, square showerhead that provided sheets of rain at a stable temperature of her choosing. She shamelessly indulged in a twenty-minute shower, one that only could've gotten better if Tristan had joined her. When she finally emerged from the bedroom, he was dressed in another goofy outfit. She was in her clothes from the night before, a true crime, given how clean she was.

"Oh, that just won't do," Tristan said, handing over her purse with one hand and holding the door open with the other. "Our first stop, the pro shop."

This was coming from a guy who prided himself on being a graduate from the clown university look. "You don't have to do that."

"Yeah," he replied, looking her over, "I do."

From the back of the Escalade that was taking them out of the city, Zoey compared herself to Cinderella, only instead of a ball gown, she was going to be adorned in ill-fitting neon plaid. When Tristan took her hand and began to trace sensual circles with his thumb over her knuckles, it was a small price to pay.

Luckily, she didn't have to make the sacrifice. After entering through the front door, Tristan led her past the raised eyebrows of the country club staff and other members, with his hand surrounding hers. He smiled in return to every greeting with a nod of his head and didn't stop until they were at the door of the pro shop. He held the door open for her, and they stepped inside.

"Good morning, Mr. Malloy!" the clerk greeted him and tried to stifle her surprise at the sight of Zoey still firmly attached to him.

"Good morning. I'd like to have my girlfriend outfitted for a day on the course, please."

He was still polite, but there was a new air about him. Maybe he was merely adapting to his surroundings, but now he sounded more authoritative than accommodating. And he called her his girlfriend. The moment set her heart fluttering again.

"It would be my pleasure, Mr. Malloy," the clerk said.

Tristan finally let go of her hand and said brightly, "I'm going to go see if I can switch up our tee time. Have fun."

He gave her a quick kiss and made for the door, adding over his shoulder, "Whatever she wants. Just add it to my account."

As the clerk profusely nodded her head and reiterated her delight at the task, Zoey took a look around the opulence and thought, *Forget Cinderella, this is right out of* Pretty Woman.

As she began to look through the racks, Zoey was also pleasantly surprised to find out that women's golf clothes were a million times more fashionable than men's.

Without Tristan in the room, the clerk's focus turned to Zoey. She gave Zoey a look up and down. Zoey did the same, making note of her name tag—ERICA. The two women pasted smiles on.

"So, what are we looking for today?"

Erica's voice was syrupy sweet and that meant only one thing. Artificial, which leads to probably bad for you.

"Something to divide my boyfriend's attention between me and his game." Zoey grinned. She normally wouldn't be so liberal with the word *boyfriend,* but she had encountered this kind of woman before.

Erica immediately walked over to the rack and pulled out a pair of black capris, presenting them to her.

"These hide a multitude of sins," Erica said.

Zoey was willing to give the woman the benefit of the doubt. After all, she was wearing her work outfit, which consisted of black pants and a white button-down.

"All my sins take place when I'm not wearing any clothes at all," Zoey replied pointedly, returning to her search of the racks. "And you see how he's dressed. I have to at least try to keep up."

Whether Erica's subsequent laugh was in response to embarrassment or appreciation of her joke, Zoey didn't care. Then her sight alit upon something.

Oh yeah. This should hit him right in the meatballs.

She pulled it off the rack and held it up for Erica to see.

"I want to start with this," Zoey stated firmly. "I don't suppose you have it in plaid?"

After Erica's initial surprise, given away by the raising of her brows, she broke out into a smile. "Afraid not. But I think I know where you're heading with this. I've got just the things to complete the look."

Sometimes all a person needs to get on board is the knowledge that you don't hate your own body. Erica gathered some other things, and the two of them went to the dressing room giggling.

When Tristan returned, almost an hour later, it was his turn to hide his astonishment, but his reaction was more of a carnal nature.

Zoey was dressed in a white pleated golf skirt that settled midthigh. She had waved off the skort version with a conspiratorial wink to Erica, who supplied her with white spandex boy short panties. It was paired with a pink polo shirt, tucked in at the waist, and a black belt. She topped it all off with knee-high socks. It was Catholic schoolgirl, golfing edition.

The sight of Tristan's jaw unhinging was priceless.

"I'm glad they had the right shoes for you" was his poor attempt at hiding it.

"I know," Zoey replied casually, forcing his attention back up her curvaceous, muscular legs. You don't hoof around New York City for almost a year without reaping some sort of reward. "I'd hate to slip and get grass stains on this white skirt."

Golf was now the last thing on her mind. By the look on Tristan's face, it had fallen down the ranks of his priorities as well.

He signed the sales slip and took Zoey by the elbow to lead her out the door.

"You should've bought ten of this outfit." He breathed seductively in her ear.

Mission accomplished.

"Can I drive the golf cart?" she asked, using her best sexy voice. "Please?"

"Of course." He smiled, picking up on it. Then he shook a stern finger at her. "But don't you dare drive it on the green. They will kick me out of the club so fast, my head will spin."

His next order of business was to cancel the use of a caddy.

"I don't normally use one," he explained. "But I thought we could use a chaperone."

"You thought wrong, mister."

"I think I can forget about trying to show off my skill. I have the funny feeling I'm about to have my worst round on record."

They loaded her rented clubs beside his in the golf cart, and they set off for the first tee.

It was slow for a Thursday afternoon at the club, with most of the dedicated members having chosen the earliest tee times. Some of them could be seen as small dots on the horizon smattered on the course. It was quiet, with the exception of the cart's low motor-running hum and intermittent birdcalls. And lush. So much rolling green, with the strategic placing of sand traps, trees, and ponds of water off in the distance. The air smelled clean and fresh. Wildlife peeked out and dashed from behind trees and out of bushes. It was easy to see why Tristan was so dedicated to the sport and the serenity it provided.

She had also forgotten how much she loved to drive. She looked over at Tristan to tell him so. He looked deep in thought.

"Don't worry. I have a license to drive a real car. This thing is a piece of cake."

"It's not that. I was just thinking that I'm supposed to have come up with some sort of nickname for you. You know, a term of endearment that only I use. Like honey or baby or darling."

"So, what's the problem?"

"All of them sound stupid and disrespectful. Belittling. Shouldn't these sorts of things come naturally?"

She stopped the cart and grabbed his hand, looking into his eyes.

"Tristan, there is nothing more endearing to me than to hear you say my name. I get butterflies inside every time you do it. If something suddenly comes to you, fine. If not, you're still giving me all the feels."

He instructed her where to stop near the first-hole tee and hopped out of the cart to grab a club, eager to get started.

"Do you mind if I just watch you for a hole or two?" Zoey asked. Not only did she want to take some time to adjust to wearing the skimpy outfit, but she also wanted to watch him in action. If he looked anything like he did in his living room the day they met, she would need a while to adjust to that too. She wasn't disappointed. First it was the precious look he got as he concentrated on the ball. Then it was the delicious way his hips and tush wiggled as he shifted his weight from one foot to the other before he swung. As he teed off and his upper body responded with the motion, she officially abandoned the notion that golf was boring. Maybe it was because he was in his element. Maybe it was the way his body twisted that reminded her of the night before. She lost sight of the ball as it rocketed through the air, mainly because she hadn't watched it. She was preoccupied with looking at him. Her excitement over driving the golf cart was all but forgotten, replaced with an entirely different desire.

At first, they sporadically encountered other golfers. Some were making their way back to the clubhouse, others moving farther away as their games progressed. Most of them were dressed in solid colors that were both neutral and matched.

"I just have to ask," Zoey said after making that observation. "What is your obsession with all the crazy outfits?"

"I think I picked it up from my grandfather. He spent most of his life in colors designated by the army, which basically meant beige or green, with the occasional camouflage. But you think I'm bad? He really made some fashion statements on the course back in his day. For such a disciplined man, golf clothes were where he cut loose."

She wondered what Tristan must have been like as a boy. He painted a picture that had her imagining waking up to a bugle every morning at dawn and being tested to see if a quarter could bounce on his bed ten minutes after that. A little towheaded Tristan, dressed in fatigues.

On their way to the third tee, she was ready. And not just to play golf.

It started with bending over in front of him to put her ball on the ground. After finally getting the ball to balance on the little tee, but before standing up, she coyly looked over her shoulder in his direction. His eyes were riveted on her backside. One of his arms was crossed over his chest, gripping the elbow of the other, his hand with a firm grab on his chin, his mouth slightly agape. She would never tire of that look.

"What do I do now?" she asked innocently.

Tristan shook his head to break the stare. He pulled a club out of her bag.

"Drivers are the most accurate, but you sacrifice distance," he explained while approaching her. "But since you're just beginning, let's start with a three wood."

"That's made of iron," she pointed out while taking it.

"I know." He chuckled. "Wood is the name of the club. They have longer shafts and rounder heads, to drive the ball farther."

"I think I just found a term of endearment nickname for *you!*"

She waited for him to catch on to the joke, thinking, *Good grief, didn't this dude's grandfather have at least one* Playboy *or* Penthouse *lying around for him to stumble across?* She knew he had caught on when he started to blush ten shades of red.

"You are not only naughty, you're dirty," he admonished her with a bashful grin.

"You have a problem with that?"

"Not in the slightest."

"If I had known just how much sexual innuendo came with golf, I would've taken an interest in the sport years ago. What do I do next?"

Tristan got serious. "While you might believe golf is all about the swinging of your arms, you really want to work your game from the ground up. Your footwork and interaction with the turf is vital. It's not all about the hands."

"You might want to rethink that in your case. Your hands can get pretty magical."

"Thanks for the compliment. I realize you want to play, but I'll feel like a complete failure if I don't at least teach you the basics. Can you keep your mind on the game for one hole, please?"

"Trust me, it already is."

Tristan narrowed his eyes, and she peered up at him with feigned innocence with hers.

"Sorry," she said. "I'll get serious."

"Good. Now you don't want to grip the club too tightly, because that would engage more of your wrist. You don't want that. What you want is more like your arms becoming an extension of the club. You don't want to break your wrists. Does that make sense?"

"Yes," she replied. She had been so busy watching his mouth, she hadn't heard a word. But she didn't want him to regret bringing her along either. Zoey stationed herself behind the ball and imitated his foot-to-foot shifting.

"You need to adjust your grip. One hand over the other, not too tight."

She shot him a knowing look.

"Spread your legs a little and keep your eye on the ball. Bend your knees a little."

He had to know that sounded downright perverted.

She put her head down to look at the ball, but when she swung the club, she closed her eyes. The end result was her looking out to see how far it went and finding it still on the tee.

"You're swinging too fast without keeping your focus on the ball. You have to hold the cock."

Zoey purposely flipped the club, sending it flying. It landed several feet away.

"Now you're just asking for it," she told him, landing her hands on her hips. It was her turn to blush.

"What?" he asked, all innocence given away by his twisted grin. "It's when you pull back your arms before the swing."

"Now I realize why guys play with guys and women with women," she mumbled while trying again, with a marginally better result.

"Good job." He congratulated her effort. Her ball had landed what looked like miles away from his.

For the sake of keeping the game from taking forever, she asked if they could take her ball and put it closer to his. What Zoey didn't know was both of them were losing interest in the game.

They scooped up her ball on the way to his and he took his next shot. She didn't bother getting out of the cart. When he made it close to the green, after sinking his put, he insisted on giving her a putting lesson. He dropped her ball about ten feet from the hole and she situated herself behind it. Then he pressed himself flush up against her from behind, his hands wrapping around hers on top of the club.

"Now when you are putting, it's more about the shoulders. You gauge how far to pull back by the distance you want the ball to travel." His mouth was only an inch away from her ear. His breath was hot and tickled the back of her neck. She was hot all over. Keeping her eye on the ball was impossible and her eyes drifted closed as she leaned back against him.

He guided her through the motion, and to her own surprise, when she forced her eyes open, the ball had disappeared.

"Look at that." He smiled into her neck before giving it a kiss, his voice and proximity setting her ablaze. "It went right in the hole. We're pretty good on the short putts."

She dropped the club and twisted herself within his arms. Her hands went to his neck and she pulled his lips to hers.

They drove to the next hole, and he promptly teed off into the trees.

"You did that on purpose," she accused him.

"Damn straight," he replied, grabbing her hand and racing for the cart, commandeering the driver's seat. "I know this course like the back of my hand."

They drove to the edge of the woods and she hastily got out with him, grabbing his hand and pulling him into the forest. They passed his ball on the way and both ignored it. When they were deep within the woods and far enough for his satisfaction, he gently steadied her against a tree and after an intense open-mouth kiss, he dropped to his knees.

This gentle man had hidden wolf tendencies, and it was driving her mad. The fact that he was just as turned on and willing to take the risk of doing this someplace where they could be caught had her throbbing all over.

He started a trail of kisses that began at the top of her knee sock, his fingers brushing against the back of her legs. Zoey grabbed onto handfuls of his hair until his head began to disappear under her skirt. Then it was all she could do to remain standing.

"Oh. My." She gasped as his fingers began to push aside the material of her boy shorts to gain better access to her. She heard his grunt of impatience, and with a forceful tug, he pulled her panties down. They pooled around her ankles. With his hands firmly gripping her bottom, he kissed her there.

"Yes, Tristan, yes." He added his tongue, and she brought a hand to her mouth to stifle the impending scream that she was sure would follow.

She heard him saying her name repeatedly through the haze that lingered after he stood back up, reaching into his back pocket. He ripped the foil packet open with his teeth and began to quickly roll on the condom. She tried to help him, but he pushed her hand away.

"No time," he groaned into her mouth while lifting her. "If you touch me, I'm done."

In the next breath, he lowered her onto his sex, thrusting himself deep inside her.

He helped her back into her panties, righted his own clothing, and brushed the bark off the back of her clothes before taking her hand, and on shaky legs, they returned to the cart.

"I can't believe you were capable of that," Zoey said when she was once again able to think rationally.

"I've overheard men talking in the locker room in the past. If half of what they're saying is true, it happens more than you think. Did I overstep?"

"It was my favorite lesson today, hands down."

"Well, you know what they say. Practice makes perfect."

"I can honestly say that right now, there is nothing I care less about than golf." The memory of what they had done was still so fresh, she was light-headed and swoony.

"I hope I didn't ruin the sport for you."

"On the contrary, I will never look at it the same way again."

"That makes two of us."

"That's really saying something. I'll take that as a compliment."

"It was certainly meant as one."

Instead of driving to the next tee, Tristan turned the cart back in the direction of the clubhouse. Zoey turned to Tristan, puzzled.

"I was only kidding before. Sort of." Zoey could feel herself blushing furiously while looking at him. He had once again left her feeling weak, in a multitude of ways. She suddenly felt shy and had trouble telling him that he had provided the most climactic experience of her life. She settled on telling him, "I love watching you play."

"Zoey, you have sapped me of all my concentration for golf. And I'm hungry, for you and for food. What do you say we head back to my place, order more pizza, and spend the rest of the day in bed?"

They were still quiet in the car on the way back into the city. But he had already changed. From the backseat of the car, he boldly placed his hand on her knee. Then he slowly let it creep up her thigh before coming to rest just under her skirt. He gently stroked her over her panties while still maintaining his gaze out the window.

"Insatiable." She wiggled then leaned over and whispered in his ear. "And really not fair."

He turned away from the window to bestow a most devilish smile and politely returned his hand to his own lap. When they got back to his place, she was going to teach him some lessons of her own to try and even the sensual score.

"Can we stop at my place, so I can pick up a few things?" Zoey asked.

"Certainly," he replied, kissing her, then gave her address to the driver.

Tristan asked the car to wait and accompanied Zoey up to the apartment. He wasn't through touching her, he was so caught up in their euphoria. Before she opened the door, he stopped to give her one more thorough kiss, and she stuck the key in the lock.

From the doorway, she saw a hulking figure standing in the middle of her living room with its back to the door. It turned around at Zoey's sharp intake of breath and began to smile.

Chapter 20

"Derek." Zoey stood the kind of straight that had Tristan taking his hand off the small of her back when she uttered the single word.

"Hi, Zoey."

"What are you doing here?" she said as the initial shock started wearing off.

Derek looked different. His eyes were clear, his posture straight. Gone was the belligerent slouch. With a congenial smile, he crossed the space between them while outstretching his hand toward Tristan.

"Hey, man, Derek Sullivan. Nice to meet you."

Another first. He was nonconfrontational in his greeting upon seeing her with another man. Tristan took his hand with a brief nod. "Tristan Malloy. Pleasure."

Tristan's manner was polite, but Zoey could feel the tension in his voice as well as in the room. After the handshake, Derek took Zoey by the shoulders and placed a light kiss to her forehead.

"I'm sorry, babe. I just couldn't wait any longer. I missed you so much. You're a sight for sore eyes."

He was saying all the right words, had struck just the right tone. It was more unnerving than anything else.

"Where's Ruth?" Zoey stammered, still trying to come to grips with what was occurring. Why hadn't she texted her some sort of warning that Derek had come to the city?

"Her and Blake left right after they let me in," Derek said. "She told me I could stay here tonight to save myself a hotel stay. She seems really happy. Maybe this guy is the one for her?"

Derek was casual in making with the chitchat, like he had no problem at all with his wife walking in, dressed in a tiny skirt, with another man. New Derek was so confusing. Zoey could feel her face start to flush again, this time with unexplained shame. Though she hadn't done a thing wrong, she couldn't bring herself to look directly at Tristan. She didn't need to see him take several steps away from her; she could feel him moving away.

"I think it's best if I leave," Tristan said gallantly. "Give you two and this reunion some time alone."

Zoey wanted to beg him to stay, to help her be strong and fearless, but the words couldn't get past the lump in her throat. Her mouth wouldn't open. All she heard was the pounding in her ears when she finally worked up the courage to turn toward him only to see his back walking away.

"Later, bro," Derek called after him. "Nice to meet you."

Once Tristan was gone, the fog started to lift and only the confusion remained. When she turned back to Derek, he was looking her up and down.

"What's with the getups?" he asked once his gaze reached her face and they made eye contact. "You two at a costume party?"

"We were playing golf," she replied slowly, so slow as to appear absentminded.

"Look at you, city girl living the high life." His attempt at humor sounded more like an insult.

She felt her backbone trying to slip back into place.

"Derek, what are you doing here?" she asked again.

"My therapist told me if I took the chance and showed up early, it would be a good gesture to show you just how much you mean to me."

"You went into therapy? Why am I just hearing about this now?"

"Because I was the one who screwed up and needed help," he replied. "It wasn't easy at first. I knew if I was going to make the changes you asked for, I wasn't going to be able to do it alone."

He sounded contrite, something that was new for him as well. But Zoey was still far from convinced.

"What angle are you working here, Derek?"

"No angle, babe. No games. When you left me, it was a real wakeup call. It sent the clear message that I needed to make some changes if I had any hope of getting you back. I passed the test for my real estate license. I already have a job waiting for me back home. Waiting for us. I want to give you all the things I promised you when we got married."

"What about your other women?"

"I flirted, okay? I flirted a lot." He sounded defensive then quickly reined it in. "And that was unfair to you. But I never slept with anyone else."

"Not even while we were apart?" she probed.

"I was as loyal as I'm sure you were." It was a perfectly designed dig to get her to back off the topic. And it worked.

"Let's not get stuck in the past," he said, real emotion starting to show. "I take full responsibility for our breakdown. In the ten months I've been sober, I've been doing a lot of reflecting. I was a rotten husband. Looking back, it's easy to see why you wouldn't want to start a family with the likes of me. I not only have you to thank for pushing me to change, but you're also the reason I did it all."

"I told you before"—she felt her own emotions start to come to life—"I'm not sure I want children."

"That's fine," he was quick to concede. "Maybe we can talk about it again once you see what a great provider I can be."

Zoey's head was spinning. It was too much, too new, too soon. He was much like the Derek she fell in love with, only more mature and accommodating. To her own surprise, she heard herself say, "Maybe."

"All I know is you told me I needed to be a different man, and I've been working hard toward that goal. I know I don't deserve another chance, but I came here because I'm strong enough to hear your decision now. I'm hoping you'll say yes. No, I'm begging you to say it. This is the last time. I swear."

Zoey had heard his speech before, more times than she could count. But he had managed to accomplish all the things she insisted he do, something she never thought possible. And he had done them quietly, without grandstanding. Took those painful steps alone toward her. For her. She thought about all the times he had called her and ended up snapping at her when she accused him. He was battling his demons, maybe trying to reach out to her for support. Now he was here, with his hat in hand and on a singular mission, to win her back.

But then there was Tristan. Sweet, sexy, chivalrous-to-a-fault Tristan. They had no real history. There had been no declarations of love, just a gradual buildup of attraction that inevitably exploded in passion. He didn't even stick around long enough to fight for her. That alone said something. He had gone through changes too, but his changes were all for and about himself. Tristan had only begun to tap into his potential. Even if he did have strong feelings for her, what were the odds that they were going to last? Didn't he deserve the opportunity to experience all that was out there? Did she really want to spend her life walking him through the paces of the modern world?

When Derek spoke up again Zoey was forced to stop thinking before she could get to her own answer.

"Look, Zoey, I know Ruth said I could stay the night, but I want to go home now. And I want you to come with me. I don't want to pressure you, but if you've given this as much thought as I have over the past year, it should be an easy choice to make. I love you so much, but more than that, I care for you and want to take care of you. I know I can be a better man with you by my side."

He had said every single thing she had always longed to hear, because he already knew all her soft spots. And he was right, there was no reason for her to wait until morning. After all the legitimate sacrifices he had made, she owed it to them both to give their marriage another chance.

"Let me gather my things," she said, without any enthusiasm.

It was close enough to yes for Derek, but he made no moves to seal it with a kiss. He didn't even try to touch her.

"I promise you won't regret it," he told her confidently. "If you make it quick, we may even make it home before midnight."

Zoey went to the bedroom to throw everything she owned into the same suitcase she had arrived with, while Derek watched TV on the futon. Her movements were systematic and almost robotic, refusing to focus on anything other than the task at hand. Until she began packing her magic bag of spices. She ran her fingers over the tattered leather and fought back an unexpected wave of tears. She'd had such optimism when she'd bought it, so many dreams she was sure she would fulfill. She shook her head, angry at herself, and zipped up the suitcase. Then she sat on the edge of the bed and pulled out her phone. She knew she didn't have much time. After texting Ruth that Derek was taking her back home, she found Tristan's number and wrote him the following:

HEY. I'M GOING BACK TO OHIO. IT'S THE RIGHT THING TO DO.

She hit SEND, watched the text get delivered, and waited. Waited for some answer, any sign of him telling her not to go. Or to think it over. Or wishing her luck. Anything to show her that he cared one way or the other. After five minutes without any response, she dragged her bag into the living room and told Derek she was ready.

Chapter 21

Three hours later, they sat side by side in the souped-up Honda Civic Derek had acquired in her absence. To Zoey they might as well have been on opposite sides of the Grand Canyon. She stared out the window and wondered if he felt the emotional distance too.

Her guess was no. The farther they drove out of the city, the more the old Derek began to peek out. He had assumed his usual driving position, reclined way too far back for comfort, his wrist propped up by the steering wheel, daring the car to waver out of his control. He was merrily droning on about all the things he had accomplished in her absence. How trying it was to work a full-time job and get his real estate license. How difficult it was to give up his old ways. How much happier he was now that he had. Simply rehashing all the same rhetoric he used to get her to go with him, only now with more self-congratulatory old Derek overtones. Then he ventured to how good she looked. That the few extra pounds she put on made her more curvy and luscious. He was really putting on the hard sell. She managed to keep up with bits and pieces of his soliloquy, nodding and smiling in the right places. The whole time, the same thought kept looping in her head. *If I made the right decision, why do I feel so lousy?*

It was unlikely she would be able to stay silent the whole eight-hour drive home without him noticing. When she finally thought up something to say, it wasn't much better. She blurted it by accident.

"I feel like I lost my best friend."

"Ruthless has the right to move on. The fact that she settled on a lawyer is hilarious. I can't wait to tell everyone back home."

Home. She wasn't heading home, she was leaving it. When had that change occurred? She knew the answer. For the first time, she was grateful that Derek was so self-absorbed, he didn't have a clue what she meant.

"Blake is a nice guy," Zoey murmured at the window.

"Only your sister could get a dude to take on a judge." Derek laughed. "He probably bangs her better than a gavel."

Some things hadn't changed. No matter how clean he looked, how handsome and well put together he now appeared, Derek was still crude. She considered the possibility of this whole ordeal being one big fraud. Would he really go to such great lengths to paint a picture of success just to claim her? Sadly, she knew the answer. In the past, Derek had often thrived on spite. Convincing her to come home might be the only victory he wanted.

Five years ago, she would've laughed at that joke. A year ago, she would've put up with it. Now, she wasn't inclined to do either.

"I've always wondered what your fascination was with my sister's sex life," Zoey pondered aloud.

Derek sat up straighter and put both hands on the wheel.

"Damn, baby, relax. It was just a joke. Or did big-city life beat the humor out of you?"

He became defensive too quickly, like she had struck a nerve. Old Derek was reappearing in record time.

"We're from Cleveland, not the outback," she snapped. "I'd like to think I would've outgrown tasteless jokes no matter where I lived."

"Point taken, *Mom*," he said sarcastically.

Zoey bit her tongue. She silently promised herself that if he so much as tried to start the motherhood conversation, she was going to open the car door and tuck and roll herself out onto the highway. She opened her window and let the warm exhaust-filled air blow through her hair.

"Do you mind?" he said, using the button on his side to reclose her window. "I've got the AC on."

They drove in silence for several miles, his knuckles now white on the steering wheel. Then he tried a different approach.

"Now that I'm going to be a real estate mogul, you'll have plenty of time to get your little business going."

Zoey could only sigh. Despite all the condescension, she knew he was trying to extend an olive branch. He was so arrogant, automatically assuming that a Realtor's license was going to be his golden ticket to riches, never dawning on him the amount of work that lay ahead of him if he had any hope of being successful. Equally depressing, she no longer had any desire to keep doing what only months ago was near an obsession. She knew the reasoning behind that disinterest as well.

"I don't think there's a market for my kind of service in Cleveland."

"Wow. I can't tell if you're being defeatist or elitist. Either way, don't beat yourself up. Not everyone has what it takes to be their own boss. You're a good worker bee though."

Derek had apparently forgotten that he hadn't held down a steady job for the majority of their marriage. He always did have a selective memory. Zoey didn't bother responding.

"Maybe it's your fancy uptown boyfriend that's made you so classy?"

Zoey remembered all their discussions that quickly turned to arguments. Only his opinion was the right one. What he didn't count on was her newfound capacity to ignore his goading.

"Maybe." She went back to staring out the window.

"You like real men. You would've been bored with that Popsicle in no time."

She turned back to Derek. "Popsicle?"

"Yeah." Derek went back to reclining in his seat, mistaking her soft-spoken demeanor for submission. "You know, like he has a stick up his ass?"

Only someone of Derek's caliber would mistake good manners for snobbishness. As he laughed at his own joke, she pictured herself wrestling the wheel from him and driving them both into a ditch. A calmness came over Zoey. It wasn't too late to rectify her situation. No need to kill anyone. All she had to do was make it to the next rest stop. She would call a cab from the bathroom and escape from a window if necessary. She didn't even need to go back to New York. Since she'd burned her bridges with Tristan, there was nothing to get excited about back in New York anyway. At any rate, she would clean toilets in a prison to keep from continuing this farce.

"If I had known that was my competition, I wouldn't have rushed to the rescue."

Zoey turned to him and tilted her head curiously. "Rescue? Really? I'm still wondering why you showed up at all."

"When Ruth called me, she told me I better hurry or I was going to lose out to someone who had turned your head."

"Seriously?" Her sister had betrayed her.

"She didn't mention that the man in question was a scrawny pretty boy. A robust girl like you needs a hard-muscled guy to stand next to, make you look proportionate. A dude with a gene pool like that will only give you chubby girls and wimpy boys."

"Stop the car."

Derek took his eyes off the road to give her a look that accompanied his now–half smile. "Say what?"

"Pull the car over, I'm getting out." Zoey replied as casually as if she were asking him to turn the car radio to a different station.

"Don't be ridiculous. We're on the turnpike. I'm

sorry about the chubby girls comment, okay? I like your cushion, it's better for the pushin'."

Zoey laughed, the kind of laughter that would've been a warning to a wiser man. She shook her head. "I don't care about that comment. Or any of the others. I don't need to worry about any children we would have. My biggest mistake was getting in this car with you. And luckily, it's the easiest one to fix. Now pull this car over before I call nine-one-one and tell them you kidnapped me."

He pulled the Honda to where the shoulder met the dirt. "You're a crazy bitch."

"That's right," Zoey said while opening the door. "I am. I'm the craziest bitch you ever laid eyes on. I can make Ruth look like a Girl Scout."

He popped the trunk and got out along with her, yelling across the car. "You're going to be sorry about this."

"Got that right. I'm already sorry. Sorry I met you."

Derek took out Zoey's suitcase, his anger and voice ramping up more with each word. "What the hell makes you think you're so perfect? You think anyone else would go through what I did to get you to come home? You're not even worth it."

Then, after taking a few steps and a windup, Derek

launched her suitcase down the embankment. He stomped back to get into his car, but right before he did, he bared his teeth and pointed a finger.

"Good luck!" he shouted from across the roof in an attempt to be heard over the passing traffic.

He got back into his car and rolled down the passenger window. Like an idiot, she took a step over to the car and peered in. "And just to set the record straight, I didn't come to New York for you. I went there for Ruth."

She could read his lips as if she couldn't hear him loud and clear. By the end they had curled up in a sneer. Even if it was a lie, there was truth behind it. She backed away from the car, standing straight up, looking off into the horizon. Even when she didn't care one whit about him, he still managed to hurt her.

With the tires screeching loud enough to be heard over the muffler and kicking up dust, he peeled away, accompanied by the sound of a car horn blaring as he merged. She saw his hand thrust out the driver's side, middle finger up. Whether it was directed at her or the honking driver was immaterial. He had managed to kill two birds with one stone.

Zoey watched his car, and the finger, until it was out of sight. Then she half stepped, half slid her way down the steep embankment, scooping up what she hoped was her own toothbrush as she passed it. Her suitcase had opened up upon landing, likely with some unzippering help from Derek before he heaved it. As she gathered up her remaining possessions from the shrubs and weeds, she began to laugh again. Never had she seen karma work so quickly.

"This is nothing less than I deserve." She pulled a pair of her panties out of a thorny bush and contemplated the ironic significance while chucking it back in the suitcase. "I never made an impulsive decision that didn't end up kicking me in the ass."

It became a game, retrieving her scattered garments, balling them up, then shooting them in the direction of the open suitcase. She wanted to take her time, because as soon as she climbed back up the small hill, she would have to get back to deciding what she was going to do next. There were only a few hours of daylight left. If she didn't find a way off the highway, she was going to be in deep trouble. She seriously doubted taxis picked up from the side of a toll road, especially when you couldn't tell them exactly where you were. Then she spied her magic bag, open with at least half the jars of spices broken in the impact, sprinkling a dust of their own on the ground. All her laughter came to an end and her eyes burned with tears she refused to shed.

How had it come to this? Only hours ago she was making love on a golf course with the man who made her feel like the most cherished, beautiful woman in the world. Now she was battling bees for what was left of her toiletries. Was there a part of her that secretly deemed her worthy of only drama and failure? She had stayed with Derek long past their relationship's expiration date. She was having trouble remembering why she married him. Had she gone to New York for adventure, or to try and watch over her sister, or for something else entirely? And what about her business? She had been so gung-ho when she started it. So much so, she curtailed all other activities to make it a success, then threw it all away to go back to Ohio.

"Heeeeyyy!" Zoey turned toward the sound coming from the highway.

Zoey squinted through the sun up the ditch. It was a woman, standing on the shoulder. At least it sounded like a woman. It was hard to tell. All she could make out for certain were a baseball cap and sunglasses. Her hands were planted on her hips. The backdrop, an eighteen-wheeler.

"You okay down there?" the figure asked.

"Yeah!" Zoey called back, hustling to gather up the rest of her things.

"Need any help?" Zoey's savior took a few steps in making her way down the embankment.

"No, I got it." Zoey zipped the suitcase closed and started dragging it back up the hill.

When Zoey reached the shoulder, she stood the suitcase up and brushed the dirt off her butt and the backs of her legs. She took a seat on the suitcase to catch her breath, finally able to take it all in. It was a woman, and a petite one at that. She was dressed in jeans and a tee shirt that upon closer inspection read KEEP CALM AND CARRY BACON. A woman after her own heart. The brunette hair under the cap was in a ponytail. She looked to be near to forty, with a cautious smile.

"Thanks for stopping," Zoey said, wiping the sweat off her brow with a dirty hand.

"I was driving by when I saw that guy make the throw. What a dick."

"Yeah. Soon-to-be ex-husbands can get pretty touchy."

"He's lucky I can't stop on a dime, or he would've been staring down the barrel of my forty-five. I got his plate number when he passed me before I turned around. You want me to call the cops?"

"Hell no," Zoey replied. "Believe it or not, this was the best-case scenario. With any luck, I'll never see him again. Ever."

"Well, all righty then. Come on, I'll give you a lift to the next rest stop. Name's Phyllis."

Phyllis motioned for Zoey to stand up, and she took the suitcase to store in the big rig's lower storage compartment. She was surprisingly strong for such a tiny woman.

"I'm Zoey. Thanks again." She knew about the dangers of accepting rides from strangers, but this was the kind of serendipitous moment that you don't take for granted.

Phyllis was not only strong, she was also wiry. While Zoey scaled the side of the truck cab like she was trying for an attempt at Mount Everest, Phyllis had already swung herself back in the saddle with the ease of a well-oiled spider monkey. She leaned way over and opened Zoey's door for her final heave-ho.

Zoey settled into the passenger seat, preparing to share space with a cloud of stale cigarette smoke, a slew of empty coffee cups, and stacks of lady porn.

But she was mostly wrong. The inside of Phyllis's cab was pristine and smelled like bubble gum. There was a cup of coffee in the cup holder, next to a liter bottle of water. Phyllis buckled her seat belt, cranked the mighty shifter into gear, and after checking that the coast was clear, the big rig jolted forward and they eased back into traffic.

"Where you headed?"

Phyllis had unwittingly asked the million-dollar question. Zoey didn't want to go to Cleveland. It wasn't just because of Derek either. Her parents would try to push her back into Derek's arms. In their eyes, marriage was for better or for worse with few exceptions. There was nothing for her back in New York either, other than a sister who had deceived her and the love she had stupidly cast aside.

"Honestly?" Zoey said. "I don't know."

"You're welcome to ride along with me for a spell. This load dumps in Detroit."

The Motor City. It was as good a place as any. "Thanks. I'm going to take you up on that, if you don't mind."

"I wouldn't've asked if I did."

From all the stereotypical things Zoey knew about truckers, Phyllis was supposed to be longing for company and conversation. But there was nothing typical about the woman who had come to her rescue. Phyllis wasn't chatty. Zoey couldn't even consider her as overly friendly. She had no interest in probing Zoey for details on how she ended up a damsel in distress. She kept her eyes on the road and her vibe screamed that she didn't suffer fools lightly. It was a safe assumption, considering she was willing to point a gun at Derek. That alone was reason enough for Zoey to like her.

"What made you want to be a truck driver?"

"I wanted to travel, but hate to fly. I figure, when I see everything there is to see here, then I'll bite that bullet."

Was her response designed to start the conversation, or end it? Zoey was too weary to analyze or worry that she needed to fill the dead air.

A Garth Brooks song began to play inside the cab, one of her mother's favorites. A random memory flashed in her head. Zoey and Ruth as children, in the backseat of their parents' minivan during countless road trips to various, usually historical family vacation destinations. The memory in question involved a trip to Williamsburg, Virginia. It was a game they played to kill time. Whenever they passed one of those big rigs, they would wait to see if the truck driver would look, then hold up one of their arms and pull it down repeatedly, a universal sign used as a request for the truck driver to sound the horn. The giggling that would result when the truck driver complied, the way they would stick their tongues out when they didn't. It was Garth on the radio when Zoey knew they had outgrown the game and Ruth switched to giving a one-finger salute to stone-faced drivers who dared to ignore them. Ruth and Derek really did have lots in common.

Ruth. Always making up her own rules, usually ruining the game for both of them in the process. The same Ruth who sided with Derek. It was more than she wanted to think about right now. Zoey opted for closing her eyes, and within minutes she was asleep.

Zoey was startled out of her nap by the sound of the truck's horn. It was a loud rapid beeping sequence, like the trucker's version of Morse code. Another truck, on the opposite side of the highway, began doing the same. It was a volley of deep, rowdy, ear-vibrating sounds that had her bolting upright in her seat. It was almost dark.

"Sorry," Phyllis said with a sideways glance. She flipped on the CB. "Nothing's wrong. That was my husband."

"You're married?" Zoey asked, still trying to gather her bearings out of the sleep cobweb.

"Yeah, he's my Bubba."

"His name is Bubba?"

"His name is Jeff." Phyllis gave a Zoey a smile. "Bubba is a little nickname that truckers call each other. Sometimes I call him Billy Big Rigger when I want to tick him off. He drives a route too. He's heading to Harrisburg, Pennsylvania."

It was the first real emotion she had displayed since picking Zoey up.

Suddenly the CB lit up and came alive. A man's deep voice rang in the cabin.

"Hey, little mamma. Is that a seat cover I saw in there?"

Phyllis pushed the button on the side of the microphone and laughed into it. "That's an affirmative. Glad to see you're wearing your glasses."

"I was getting worried about you, was afraid you got bit by a bear in the bushes. I expected to see you about an hour ago at the split."

"Yeah, I was helping a damsel in distress. Say hi to Zoey."

"Hi, Zoey." Jeff obediently complied.

She pushed the button and the microphone in Zoey's direction.

"Hi, Jeff."

"Keep an eye on my girl there. Make sure she's not having any shutter trouble."

"Okay," Zoey said, without having the slightest clue what she had agreed to.

Phyllis brought the CB handset back to her own mouth. "So, yeah, the only thing in the bushes for me today was a snake in a roller skate."

Zoey didn't need much clarification there. She had an excellent idea of just who the snake was.

"Bet you showed him a thing or two." Jeff added a laugh of his own.

"That's a negatory. Didn't get the chance."

"The Lord was with him today."

"Or the devil. How you doing, Bubba?"

"Had to mash the motor after some road-rager went greasy-side up. Had me brake-checking for miles. Luckily, the coop was all locked up so I saved some quality time. I'll make it to the yard tonight, but might miss the lumpers. I'll fingerprint that shit myself to get out of there."

"Flex those muscles, handsome. Me and seat cover here are going to pull into the next rest-a-ree-a and fill up on some go-go juice."

Zoey could hardly contain her glee at the exchange taking place. It was true, truckers did have a language all their own. She wasn't sure exactly what they were saying, but it was every bit as amusing as she'd hoped it would be. She was, however, pretty sure that she was the seat cover.

"Be careful they don't confuse you two for a couple of lot lizards."

Phyllis let loose a hearty laugh. "Fat chance. You be careful out there now, ya hear? This life ain't no fun without you."

The last thing Zoey heard, before Phyllis turned the CB off, was Jeff saying, "Love you, baby girl."

"That was amazing." Zoey giggled, completely enthralled.

Phyllis released a much more subdued laugh, shaking her head, and said with true affection, "He's been waiting for that since we knew we were going to pass each other. It makes his day when I play along. And he really gets off talking like that when he knows there's a captive audience. He's such a goofball. I only turn the radio on when I pass him, or I'm stuck in traffic."

"I figured you would have it on all the time."

"Honey, this is the twenty-first century. We use cell phones the same as everyone else."

"What the heck is a lot lizard?"

"A prostitute that works lined-up rigs at a rest stop."

"Oh," Zoey said. "They really have those?"

Phyllis graced Zoey with a look that translated her disbelief that a person could be so naive. "Yeah. They're also referred to as commercial company. Guy ones are called male buffalo."

Zoey may have been ignorant, but it didn't curtail her fascination. In fact, it added to it.

They exited at the ramp into the rest stop and slowly pulled into the lanes to get gas. Phyllis swung down from the cab to deal with the go-go juice. Zoey carefully got out to make a beeline for the bathroom on the other side of the parking lot, keeping an eye out for any sign of lot lizards on the way.

"How long have you two been married?" Zoey asked from her side of the table after they met up at the stop's main building and ordered some burgers and fries from the Burger King.

"Almost twenty years. Probably lasted that long 'cause of all the time apart."

"I guess absence makes the heart grow fonder?"

"It probably sounds unconventional to most folks. But it works for us."

"People need to mind their own business."

"Hallelujah, sister."

They finished eating and went back to the truck, where Phyllis took a nap and Zoey mostly kept watch for any sign of the activity Phyllis alluded to. It was a lizard- and buffalo-free night, and Zoey was mildly disappointed. As soon as Phyllis woke up two hours later, they were back on the road.

"I log a crap-ton of miles during the nighttime hours," Phyllis said.

Zoey stayed with Phyllis for three days, stopping at countless greasy spoons and truck stops along the way. They made for good traveling companions. Phyllis had an aversion to extraneous small talk, although she would swear a blue streak when reckless idiots cut her off. Jeff checked in with his wife several times a day, mostly by phone. It was heartwarming to see Phyllis's softer side during those conversations.

Zoey let her phone battery die and never bothered to recharge it. She had nothing to say. To anybody.

Zoey was finally able to hear herself think. During the days, she watched hundreds of miles of scenery fly by the passenger window. It was different from the road trips she had taken as a child. This time, there was no final destination to get excited about reaching, just miles of open road. She tried to associate it with where she was in her life. All her roads were open. Now she just had to choose one.

After they left Detroit, Zoey insisted on treating Phyllis to a night in a nice hotel, mostly because she was starting to get a backache from all the sleeping she did sitting up and she was desperate for a good shower. She got them separate but adjoining rooms, saying both of them were probably ready for a little privacy. Phyllis didn't argue.

They showered and met up to head down to the hotel's restaurant for a good meal. Zoey did a double take. Phyllis was dressed in a flowery sundress with a cropped jacket. Her hair was down around her shoulders in waves, and she had applied some lipstick. She looked adorable.

"I know." Phyllis grinned. "I clean up nice."

They sat over prime rib and a bottle of wine, both of them savoring a meal that wasn't fast food.

"I'm looking forward to getting home," Phyllis said during dessert. "I haven't been in the same room with Jeff in almost a month. That's not to say I'm not going to appreciate the hell out of that bed upstairs tonight."

"Do you ever get lonely?" Zoey replied.

Phyllis was thoughtful for a moment. "Sometimes. Not too often. I like my own company. And you know, there is a huge difference between being lonely and alone. Both serve a purpose. When you're alone, you can listen to what your heart really has to say without other people's opinions getting in the way. You just have to be strong enough to live your truth after you hear it. And you can be in a room full of people and still be lonely."

For a woman of few words, Phyllis really knew how to drive a point home. Zoey took the statement and reflected on how it applied to her own life. Was it a fear of loneliness that kept her with Derek as long as she did? After all, she didn't have to move to New York to get rid of him. She could've crossed the bridge and moved to Cleveland. But at the time, she just couldn't bear the thought of running into Derek and having him see her struggling.

And was it a fear of loneliness that kept her as

Ruth's roommate? She knew the kind of life Ruth led. It was easier to wallow in disapproval than strike out on her own.

Which brought her to Tristan. It was likely she was so gung-ho about making him over because she projected her own fear of being lonely onto him. No, that wasn't true either. He may have started out alone, but it was clear he had gotten lonely. It's what made him reach out to her in the first place. Their backstories might have been different, but a lot of their motives were the same.

"I think I'm ready for you to drop me off," Zoey stated with conviction.

"Good," Phyllis replied with a grin. "Because I was getting ready to kick you out. I like you and all, but it's time to get back to your own way of life."

"Thanks for letting me ride along. I think I just needed the time to get my head on straight."

"Did it work?"

"I think it did."

"Where do you think you're going to land?"

Zoey was able to answer without hesitation. "New York City. I'm not sure if it's my final stop, but I have some apologies to make there. And a fight to have."

Chapter 22

There was only one other time Zoey had forgotten to return a key. The night she met Tristan. There was no indecision about what she would do with the key she kept this time. After busing her way back to New York, she let herself in to lie in wait for Ruth. She weighed the possibility that tonight might turn out like that time in middle school when they both ended up with missing chunks of hair and temporary bald spots.

The apartment already looked different to her since she had left it. It was tidy. No dishes in the sink, no random garments on the floor. There wasn't a single piece of evidence that any partying had taken place.

Zoey plugged in her phone and turned it on while she waited. The only calls she had received during her sabbatical were job opportunities with deadlines that had passed. Figures. There were no texts at all.

Ruth came in, hours after she would've gotten off work. Blake was behind her.

"Zoe." Ruth showed little surprise at finding Zoey perched on the edge of her futon. "Where have you been?"

"Worried about me, were you?" Zoey replied. "I'm sure Derek called you the minute after he shot-put my suitcase."

Blake interjected with a judicial "You ladies have a lot to talk about, so I'm going to cut out." He gave Ruth a quick kiss. "Call me later."

"Derek did call and told me all about it. It gave me one more chance to call him a shit gibbon," Ruth said as she closed the door behind Blake. Then she asked, "If you didn't want to go with him, then why did you?"

"Who are you to question me when you need to explain why you told Derek to hurry up and get here?"

Ruth didn't try to mount a defense. "To get you to make a damn decision."

"How can I make one of those if you're busy sabotaging me? Your loyalty has always been with Derek! You've been meddling since the day I left him."

"Maybe it's time you took your own inventory. Nothing reeks of meddling and misguided loyalty more than your little experiment with Tristan."

"Leave Tristan out of this," Zoey growled. It was bad enough Ruth was right.

"Which, by the way, you weren't honest about *at all*."

Ruth didn't seem angry, which succeeded in making Zoey all the more frenzied.

"What's the matter, afraid you were going to lose out on some action? Maybe you secretly harbored feelings for Derek all along too. I'll bet it was you who gave him my cell phone number in the first place."

Ruth refused to be baited. "You see what you're doing here, right? I'm not going to let you deflect your way into making this about me. Don't you think you owed it to yourself to see the best Derek had to offer and then make a move in any direction? Don't you think you owed it to Tristan?"

"I said leave Tristan out of this!" Zoey's guilt exploded out of her in a shout.

"You don't get to control this fight, Zoe, like you try to control everything and everyone else!"

"Control you? Don't make me laugh. I wish! I've spent the majority of my life cleaning up after all your messes!"

"Oh yeah? Well, if I'm the one who is so messed up, why are you the one who's homeless after picking all your shit up off the highway?"

The shouting stopped. Zoey's anger deflated and she wilted back onto the couch and dashed at the tears that suddenly threatened to roll down her cheeks. She wasn't just homeless, she also felt terribly alone. So much for Phyllis's theory.

"I didn't do what I did to hurt you, Zoe," Ruth said quietly, sitting down next to her. "But you know what I think? I think you get so involved with everyone else's life to avoid taking a risk with your own."

"Oh my gosh, you won the fight, isn't that enough? You have to kick me when I'm down?" Zoey jokingly sniffed.

Ruth wrapped a comforting arm around Zoey's shoulders. "I'm just trying to clear the air. Explain my motives. That is what you came here for, right?"

Zoey nodded weakly, not trusting herself to speak for fear of bawling.

"I never understood why you stuck with Derek as long as you did. I hated him. He's such a dog. I never told you, but he hit on me before you two got married. Who does that?"

"Believe it or not, I'm not the least bit surprised," Zoey said. She had never voiced her suspicions on that subject to Ruth. But Derek's wandering eye was common knowledge. If this was Ruth's idea of clean air, Zoey was going to need a gas mask.

"Everyone in town knew what a jerk he had turned into. But if he was your choice, that makes him family and I have to support you. And there's nothing wrong with that. Who am I to judge how two people navigate their relationship? I just tried to keep my distance from him and kept the lines of communication open with him to help you. And yes, it was me that gave Derek your cell phone number."

"You lied to me." Zoey wept.

"I did. And I'm sorry about that. But you kept harping about him pressuring you to start a family. I kept thinking, *That's just a smoke screen.* If you're so hell-bent on proving your point about your body being yours, then don't get pregnant. It really is as simple as that. There are only about a dozen ways to prevent pregnancy that don't require the man's participation. But it's not enough for you to just take control of your own life, you have to have some approval or recognition from other people in order to do it. I took all your waffling and excuses to mean that deep down you still cared for Derek."

"You're probably right," Zoey was forced to admit. "Not about my feelings for Derek, about the smoke screen. I wanted so much for him to be the person I initially fell in love with. Mom and Dad stuck together, grew together."

"It takes two people, working full-time at it, to make a relationship work. And Dad wasn't a hound dog. But their marriage isn't really our business, is it? You had finally come into your own with the cooking thing. You were seeing some real success. But every time you leaped forward, there was Derek, on the phone, making you take two steps back. I would've given anything for you to show Derek the door, so I made that judgment call. You needed to be pushed to decide, instead of hiding here."

"You did the exact same thing you accuse me of, you do realize that?"

"I do. That makes the score meddling Ruth one, Zoey a hundred."

"Well played," Zoey said. "Only your score is two. You also got Derek to drive up here."

"True. But I was sure once you saw that you were able to feel desirable again, it would give you the strength to finally show Derek the door. And I had no idea Derek was going to go full throttle in his attempt to make a good impression. He really should've been an actor. What an asshat."

They sat together in silence, Ruth's arm still across Zoey's shoulder. It was the first time that Zoey could recall feeling like the little sister. Overwhelmed, Zoey put her face in her hands and let the tears flow until they were little more than shuddering sobs. Her sister was the only person who she ever let see her cry. Ruth waited until Zoey was all cried out before speaking again.

"You changed a lot after Tristan entered the picture. You started being much more fun after meeting him. You two are way more alike, starting with being ethical, to a fault. At the very least, he got you to venture out of this apartment for something other than work."

Zoey picked her head up, not sure if her sister was just trying to lighten up the mood and get her to stop crying.

"Ugh. Tristan. I'm afraid I blew that one right out of the water."

"I was hoping that's where you'd been all this time. Hiding out at his place."

"No. I went to Detroit with a trucker named Phyllis."

Zoey had finally achieved the impossible. She had managed to shock her sister.

"Stop it," Ruth said, her eyebrows high in disbelief.

"No, it's true. She scraped me up off the highway. My guardian angel drives eighteen wheels and carries a loaded gun."

"I'm so disappointed. I wanted desperately to believe after you didn't come back here that it was because you guys had patched things up."

Zoey shook her head sadly. "A guy doesn't need to be a social guru to know breaking a relationship off in a text means it's really over."

Zoey had known all along that Tristan would do exactly what he did. He stepped aside. Maybe he was simply too gentle. But that didn't mean he deserved to be cast aside so callously.

"You are so good at being there for everyone else, maybe it's time you start doing for yourself. I don't know what happened between you two, but I do know you. I know you can live with whatever the outcome is if you try to make it right. And that is the last piece of advice I am going to give you."

They sealed their reconciliation with a hug and Zoey's vow to stay out of Ruth's affairs moving forward.

"I promise to keep my nose out of your business," she said. "But when disaster befalls you because of some dumb-ass decision, can I say I told you so?"

"Only if you're looking to start wearing dentures," Ruth replied with a squeeze and a laugh.

Zoey started to laugh as well, but she took Ruth's advice to heart.

"I see Blake hasn't gotten to all your rough edges yet."

"Of course he did. Maybe they're just the parts he likes best."

Zoey looked to Ruth for any sign that she was being tested in the art of minding her business. Ruth's subsequent grin confirmed she was.

"Which brings me to the in-other-news department. You're still homeless, unless you can afford the rent here on your own. Blake is convinced I'd make an excellent litigator. He talked me into going back to school and then law school. He offered to let me move in with him to save some money. I'm not about to show him my bank statement, but I still said yes."

Zoey couldn't believe her own ears. "Is this another test?"

Ruth smiled. "Afraid not. My party days are over, at least for the time being. Blake makes it sound pretty great. And who knows? Maybe I'll take domesticity on a test drive."

"Isn't this all a bit sudden?"

"I've kissed a lot of frogs, little sis. I know a prince when I see one. Now why don't you take a cab uptown and try to win back yours?"

Chapter 23

As soon as the door opened, there was a brief spark of surprise in Tristan's eyes, then . . . nothing. She wasn't foolish enough to think he'd be happy to see her, but she wasn't prepared for him to look so aloof either.

"Tristan," Zoey said in a rush, in the unlikely event he was going to slam the door. "I had to come and apologize. Face-to-face."

"There's nothing for you to be sorry for," he replied, opening the door wider to let her in.

"There certainly is. Whether you are aware of it or not, breaking up with someone in a text message is about as low as a person can go."

He was working overtime to keep from meeting her eyes. "There was a lot going on. I could tell you were reeling."

Zoey knew he would be polite and understanding. His empathy was one of his most admirable traits. At this particular juncture, it was heartbreaking. She wanted to throw herself in his arms, kiss him until his lips turned blue, but she didn't dare. He was standoffish, rightly so. She had hurt him, and it was evident. "I wanted to try and explain. . . ."

Her words trailed off. All the rehearsing she had done on the way over was for naught after taking one look at him. There was no good explanation for what she had done, other than a knee-jerk reaction based on a mistaken sense of duty to a marriage that should've ended a long time ago.

"You don't have to explain why you went back to your husband," Tristan stated, turning his back on her and walking down the hall. "But I'd be lying if I said I didn't wonder what you're doing here now."

"After Derek tossed my stuff onto the highway, I took a little detour back to the city. Rode shotgun in a big rig for a couple states."

Tristan turned back to her again. His lips twitched into what was almost a smile. Maybe a touch of sympathy. Then he went back to aloof, turning on his heel without asking her anything further.

"It was a lady trucker, just so you know," she explained.

"Thanks for clearing that up," he said. Just when

did he start applying sarcasm to his sentences? Zoey's heart sank. Her being here was only making it worse.

His apartment was spotless as always. Conspicuous by its absence was all of the Rock Band equipment in his living room. Further evidence that she had crushed him. She began to prattle in her effort to make amends.

"I knew inside of three hours after getting in a car with him that I had made an awful mistake. When Derek showed up clean and sober, I thought that I didn't have a choice. I stupidly felt that I had to hold up my end of the bargain. He had done everything I wanted. It wasn't until we were alone that I finally realized he hadn't changed at all. Not on the inside." The words sounded lame to her own ears.

"No, Zoey. You don't get to take all the blame. And that's not just me being noble either. If I hadn't held back on telling you how I felt about you, we could've spent that time cementing our relationship and you might have made a different choice."

His words were clipped, his tone biting. They had a distinct ring of finality to them. He wasn't going to accept her changing her mind. He didn't really go out of his way to accept her apology. He kept shuffling things around, refusing to look at her directly for more than a second. She had hurt him so badly he was back to his own version of solitary confinement.

But he hadn't asked her to leave, so there was still a glimmer of hope.

She followed Tristan to his library. One half of the room was stacks of full boxes and empty shelves. The other half, empty boxes to fill. He swept a handful of books off a shelf and began arranging them in the closest box.

When the books had been standing straight up, wedged together on the shelves, their spines looked sturdy, ageless. Upon closer inspection, many were weathered. Book covers and jackets had faded on some. Yellowed pages in danger of becoming unglued from fragile, brittle spines on others. They were similar to their owner, hiding their vulnerability beneath an exterior of even temperedness.

"You're getting rid of your library?"

"Yes. I don't know why I brought them." Tristan gave a half laugh. "They're turning out to be the most tedious part of my packing."

"You brought them because they hold your memories." The meaning behind his words were slow to register.

"You're right, there were many times they gave me comfort. I could've kept them at Paradise Cove. The place is just sitting there until I decide what to do. Now that I've made that decision, this seems like a pointless exercise."

"You're going back?"

"I can't stay here," he said wistfully.

"I'm so sorry. This is all my fault. If I hadn't intervened . . ."

"Oh no, Zoey. Don't look at it like that."

"Then tell me how to look at it," she pleaded. "Enlighten me."

He paused, and for a split second, his look softened. When he spoke again, his words were measured, nearly clinical. "My grandfather used to say, 'It's okay to quit any job, but you have to master it first.' It's easy to abandon something out of fear. But in doing so, you could be missing out on something spectacular. If you learn all you need to and still want to walk away, you're making an educated decision. When we met, I was paralyzed, terrified to take a step in any direction. Your friendship gave me the strength to take a chance. I'm glad I did."

"We turned out to be so much more than friends, Tristan." She could feel an anger starting to build at the way he was trying to sweep aside what had happened between them. "So now you're just going to pack it all in and call it quits?"

"Why not? It worked for you."

If his intention was to sting, he had succeeded. But at least he was showing signs of some spirit. And that he wasn't over her, not by a long shot.

"It most definitely did *not* work for me. Why do you think I'm here?"

"To make amends? Ease a guilty conscience, maybe? Either way, you can relax. I'm not holding any ill will. I accept your apologies. Now that the matter is settled, I hope you don't mind showing yourself out. The movers are coming at the end of the week and I still haven't started packing up the kitchen."

The kitchen. The center of where their friendship, as well as their relationship, had started. Had he brought up the kitchen on purpose?

"I could stick around and help?" she offered.

"Not necessary." His reply was brusque and immediate.

Zoey was exhausted from trying to always stay one step ahead. But if there was one thing she had gotten good at, it was fighting. Despite all the things she had helped teach him, it was the one lesson she had neglected. Not anymore. She owed him that much. She owed it to herself.

"For the love of God, would you show some blasted emotion for once in your life?!?"

And to her surprise, he did. He slammed the books he was holding into the box and his voice rose with every word until he was near to shouting. "What would you like me to say, Zoey? That I loved you and you shattered my heart? Because you did. What you did to me was worse than the hooker in Vegas. You gained my trust. All of it. Then you tossed me aside, something you swore to me you wouldn't do. You told me your marriage was over but he shows up and you kicked me to the curb!"

When he was done with his rant, he was heaving. And though she was left stunned, she still wasn't finished. "Well, I didn't see you sticking around to fight for me!"

He had lowered his voice, was already back in control. With sorrowful eyes, he said, "I don't own you. I said I should leave and you let me. I was completely blind-sided. Next thing I know, I'm getting a text that you're gone. How many times do I have to be kicked in the teeth?"

She wasn't as good a fighter as she thought. This made twice in one day that she had lost an argument with a single statement. The only difference here was, Zoey refused to let him see her cry.

"Tristan," she began, surprised by the shakiness in her voice. "I'm here now. I'm here because I love you. I love you for every single thing you are. Goofy clothes, bad hair, I adored it all. And I'm truly sorry I let the surprise at seeing Derek lead me into making a wrong decision. But I'm human and old habits die hard. I've spent a lifetime doing what I thought was expected of me. And I know you're hurt right now, but I refuse to believe that higher forces brought us together only to have this be the end."

With each heartfelt word she spoke, his eyes got glassier, and by the time she was finished, they were brimming with tears. She wanted to embrace him, but she didn't dare.

"I used to tell myself it was higher forces that brought us together too," he confessed, a single teardrop rolling down his cheek. "I wanted to change, prayed for it. Every move I tried to make only left me feeling more helpless, more afraid to trust. When I called you, I prayed that if I could just make one good friend, it would make all the difference. And when I felt an instant attraction to you, I got scared all over again. Because of you, and your willingness to help me, I was able to take those first steps out of the dark. How could I not forgive you? You saved me."

They had made such a muddle of things, all while trying to do the right thing.

"I guess when it comes to matters of the heart, truth is the right way to go. And if I was being brutally honest, I would've admitted I felt something shift the night we met too. How many times in your life are you lucky enough to meet someone who feels the same way you do? I wish I had told you how I felt when I started feeling it. I wish I hadn't tried to change you. I wish I had joined you. You were perfect the way you were. You still are."

"Oh no." He was quick to contradict. "I wouldn't have traded that experience for anything. I never felt so alive or laughed so hard as when you were introducing me to the world."

"Then can't we move past this? Can't you change your mind and stay?"

Tristan slowly shook his head, his eyes drinking her all in, filled with the need for her understanding. "I don't want to. I've experienced this life as much as I care to. It isn't for me. I want to go home."

"I get that," Zoey said, trying to curb the misery. Despite them baring their souls and the connection they had, it wasn't enough.

"I used to think my hasty departure from the island was to escape the ghosts of my grandparents. And Paradise Cove was indeed their dream. I never had to make it mine, but I felt an obligation to. I think I still do. And I love it there. I miss it. I'm so grateful to you for everything you did to show me the big city. I can make this decision with no regrets. I'm not missing anything, except the rat race."

"I get that too. It's the right call." Without realizing it, Zoey had begun to take books off the shelves and fill an empty box. An unconscious attempt to keep busy so that she wouldn't have to deal with how to move forward in her life without him. "None of it means I can't help you pack. Maybe we can share one last pizza."

"Lady, you've got yourself a deal."

They resumed packing up the books and the silence was comfortable, broken up sporadically when she discovered books she knew.

"Your grandmother really had a thing for Jackie Collins and Rosemary Rogers."

"Those were definitely her favorites."

Zoey struggled to keep the conversation light, when she longed to beg him to stay. He had made his decision and it was based on all the right reasons. To lay a guilt trip on him wouldn't be fair. He wasn't saying much either, a sign she took to mean he was having a difficult time as well. But she wanted to remember him confident and sure. She loved him enough to plaster on a brave face.

When she started with a fresh section of books, Zoey pulled one off the shelf and literally hugged it to her, before holding it out to show him.

"*The Joy of Cooking*. It's the first cookbook my parents gave me. I set it on fire by accident when I put it too close to the stove." She laughed at the memory while fanning the pages. "A pot boiled over and caused a flare-up and POOF! Singed pages soufflé."

When she looked at him again, Tristan was studying her. Zoey started to blush. She would miss that look and everything that came after it.

"What's the first thing you're going to do once you get back?" she said, to get her mind off it.

"Wow. I almost don't know where to start. Paradise Cove is going to undergo a complete remodel. I'm going to modernize it and reopen it as a luxury resort, maybe with a spa."

"That's pretty ambitious."

"I know! But if I can put people to work, that has to be a good thing, right?"

She couldn't hold back the sigh. How rare was a person who always thought about the good he could do? She wondered if he had any idea just how special he was.

"I was looking to hire someone to help with that," he continued. "A right-hand man, if you will. Only it doesn't have to be a guy. Someone with good organizational skills and attention to detail. And preferably who likes to cook."

His intention slowly dawned on her as he continued to stare. "I think I know someone who fits that bill."

He gave her a grin and a wink, which was all she needed to rush to him, in perfect timing with the opening of his arms to welcome her back into them. His mouth crashed down onto hers and his arms wrapped around her.

"What the hell took you so long to ask?" she scolded him when he finally let her up for air.

"My finesse needs work. And I didn't want to pressure you. And as soon as you walked through the door, I had made up my mind you were coming with me, even if I had to kidnap you."

"Gotta love those higher forces at work." She kissed him again. Nothing would ever feel as good as being in his arms.

"With you by my side, I feel like I could conquer the world and at the same time no longer need to."

"Isn't it funny how those things work?"

He started to sway side to side with her still tightly in his grasp. "I can't wait to spend all our days and nights together, dancing and playing Rock Band. Maybe smoking some pot."

"You're getting a little more modern every day." She allowed him to dance her around the library floor until they were both dizzy from the twirling, and the joy.

He continued to hold her close and stared down into her jubilant eyes, brushing the hair off her forehead.

"I will love you forever, Zoey. You're my one. My only."

Zoey thought she might start to swoon. Before he could recapture her mouth with his, a frown began to furrow her brow. One he noticed immediately.

"What's the matter?"

"There's still my feelings about starting a family. I love you so much, but that hasn't changed. I can't promise that it ever will."

Tristan set her at arm's length and gave her a tender smile. Then he let her go and struck a perfect Steven Tyler pose. "A baby would cramp my vicious style."

She giggled, and his smile got wide. Then he returned to being serious. He slid closer to her and brushed his knuckles across her cheek before gently tilting her chin up to meet his penetrating gaze.

"Zoey," he said reassuringly. "I've said it before, it's your body, your baby. Between the work that I do and all you did to enlighten me, I've seen enough of this world to make a valid argument for either side. As long as I have you, I have everything I need."

In the end, it was Tristan who taught Zoey the most important lessons. About what love really looked like and how it was supposed to be shown. It was the unwavering, unflinching ability to support a partner throughout their changes. Or no changes at all.

Epilogue

One year later . . .

It was the easterly trade winds that allowed the breezes in St. Croix to blow cool and kept the humidity low. On the return from her morning walk on the beach, Zoey turned her face toward them.

They had been there only a week before she had drawn two conclusions. Tristan must have been in the darkest stages of grief when he left this beautiful oasis with its sweeping vistas and tropical waters that came in every color blue she could imagine. And she didn't care if the cold never nipped at her ears or nose again.

The island wasn't the desolate place she first imagined when he told her about it. It had all the comforts of the mainland, including a Kmart and an OfficeMax. But as they got closer to the property, it was easy to see why Tristan had grown up so isolated. It was quiet and secluded. She could see no reason why his grandparents would ever have wanted to leave it.

When they first arrived, Paradise Cove was in a minor state of disrepair. The people Tristan paid to watch over the place did their best. But it was already weathered when he left, and without a steady stream of funds, the maintenance was minimal. Zoey thought about those first nights they spent chasing out geckos that scurried across the tile floors after taking up residence in the cupboards and closets. Not quite as amusing was the mongoose she found in a bathtub. But her hero assured her that it was more scared of her, and she believed him.

Tristan spent their first night showing her around St. Croix, and then the two of them hit the ground running. Within days of their arrival, a contractor he had hired from the mainland arrived, and not long after that, local workers appeared every day, ready to get to work. There were times Zoey was certain Tristan was employing every able-bodied worker in town.

They worked hard as well. Side by side and room by room, they revitalized every square inch of his grandparents' legacy, careful to preserve the intimacy that drew them to the place to begin with. Except the kitchen, which Tristan insisted be upgraded with every modern convenience imaginable until the original structure was unrecognizable and the only part left intact was the original frame. Tristan wanted the new kitchen to be a place for people to gather, not merely someplace to cook food to be carried off to another room. Zoey couldn't agree more. She had always said old habits were hard to break. As soon as the kitchen was fully functional, they were cooking for all the people who helped work on the house.

In those early days before the workers arrived and the big house was constantly abuzz, Zoey lovingly roamed the premises in search of the spirits of his grandparents, a sign telling her they approved of her being there. She imagined her husband as a boy, running up and down the halls and splashing in the nearby surf. A young lad in Bermuda shorts with tanned limbs, and hair just a tad too long. The kind his grandfather would always say needed to be cut.

They had married, in a simple ceremony performed by a local judge on a palm-fringed beach exactly three months after they arrived. Two weeks earlier, her divorce decree from Derek arrived via FedEx. She never had the misfortune of having to deal with Derek again after he left her on the side of the Pennsylvania Turnpike. Whether it was that he didn't care or that Tristan's lawyer scared him into signing the papers, she would never know. Tristan secretly had a magnificent gazebo built during the eight-day waiting period for their marriage license.

"Money talks," he reminded her with a grin, not sounding the least bit guilty for abusing his position.

Now Paradise Cove was all but finished, but the idea of filling it with tourists had lost its luster. They attributed that change of heart to being newlyweds. In December, Tristan spent his half hour doing keystrokes on his program and by January he didn't need to worry about customers again.

Zoey suggested that they run Paradise Cove the same way his grandparents had, by keeping it open for people they knew and loved. When he reminded her that he didn't really know anybody, she lovingly reminded him that she had five siblings and he better get ready to be known.

Tristan gave Zoey a few more golf lessons. They used better discretion, but she would talk so dirty to him when he tried to instruct her, they still had yet to make it past the sixth hole.

As Zoey neared the house, she could hear the familiar sound of Aerosmith blasting. Tristan was enjoying his morning session of Rock Band, before guests started to arrive and things got hectic. She quickened her pace to get inside, hoping she wasn't too late. Tristan had long since abandoned his leather pants, citing the heat. That didn't hinder her desire to watch him put on the show, since now he did all his concerts shirtless. His golden tan and rippling muscles more than made up for it. He had let his hair grow longer again, which added to the overall rock star vibe.

She dashed past the artwork that adorned the hallways, still taking a second to appreciate her favorites, and found him in the great room, guitar in hand, whammy bar being shaken hard enough to break. He was biting into his lower lip, his face twisted in rock-'n'-rolling concentration. She stood as close as she could without him noticing her and watched, wondering for the umpteenth time just how she managed to get so lucky. She fisted sweaty palms against the skirt of her cotton sundress and enjoyed the familiar tingle that coursed through her.

As if he could feel her presence in the room, as soon as the song was over, he stopped and turned in her direction. He put down the guitar and smiled his way over to where she stood to give her a proper kiss.

"Good morning, Mrs. Malloy. You ready for some breakfast?"

He never did settle on a personal term of endearment to call her and she found out that the only thing better than hearing him call her Zoey was the way he had taken to addressing her since they wed.

They walked together arm in arm to their marvelous kitchen. Zoey pulled a plate of mangoes, papaya, and banana figs out of the fridge, but wrinkled her nose when he asked her if she wanted eggs. Tristan didn't press her and pulled a box of Lucky Charms out of the pantry, setting it in front of her where she had taken a seat at the island. It was her current obsession, consuming bowls of it a day, sometimes pulling handfuls right out of the box.

"How about some cheese?" he asked. "A little bit of protein wouldn't be a bad thing. We've got a long day ahead."

"Swiss sounds good." She brightened at the thought and popped a chunk of mango into his mouth as he passed her.

"You ready for today?"

Zoey laughed. "I know most of these people. I think the better question is, are *you* ready?"

"As ready as I'm going to get. Do you think they'll like me?"

"Ruth and Blake have been singing your praises since the last time they were here. They're not just going to like you. They are going to love you. But not nearly as much as I do."

He rattled off his checklist. "The caterers will be here at ten to start setting up. Flowers show up at eleven. Your parents, brothers, and sisters arrive at noon and Blake's mother at two. The bride, groom, and best man get in at four thirty, and I've got the cars ready to pick them all up. The maid of honor, of course, is already here."

He stopped to give her one of his sexy wink-smile combos and added, "So is the flower girl."

Zoey caressed her still mostly flat belly. "Excuse me, this could very well be the ring bearer."

"I can't wait to find out," he said, moving closer and placing his hand over hers. "You feeling okay?"

She smiled warmly. "Never better."

Higher forces and self-preservation are powerful things, Zoey had come to realize with a shock. After a spontaneous, mutually wild night when passion over-ruled protection, and as her cycle got later and her symptoms began to show, she didn't fill with dread, like she had been so sure she would. She filled with indescribable wonder. But her views had started shifting long before then. There was so much beauty here, so much peace and joy, she thought it was a shame to waste it. When she told Tristan the news after having her suspicions confirmed, he curtailed any real excitement and instead sincerely started weighing their options, including his getting a vasectomy.

"If you want to stop at one, I can make sure you don't have to face this kind of decision again," he said, holding her gently in his arms, as if she'd suddenly become fragile.

It brought her to tears. There wasn't a selfish bone in his body. A piece of his beautiful soul was already growing inside her, and there was only one thing she wanted to do.

"We don't need to think about that right now," she told him with shiny, red-rimmed eyes they both blamed on hormones. "And on the bright side, for the next six or seven months, we can have all the unprotected sex we want."

"Yay! Unprotected sex!" He whooped, kissing her tummy then lowering his voice. "Good morning, little one."

They'd been having unprotected sex daily and he'd been doting on her ever since, something she didn't think was possible. He was already a first-class doter.

That day and that revelation struck her like a bolt of lightning. Her worries about having children were just another self-erected roadblock to detour her away from the path she was destined to travel. The path that led her to Tristan. And Tristan was her home.

HARPER LUXE

THE NEW LUXURY IN READING

We hope you enjoyed reading
our new, comfortable print size and found it
an experience you would like to repeat.

Well — you're in luck!

HarperLuxe offers the finest in fiction and
nonfiction books in this same larger print size and
paperback format. Light and easy to read, HarperLuxe
paperbacks are for book lovers who want to see
what they are reading without the strain.

For a full listing of titles and
new releases to come, please visit our website:

www.HarperLuxe.com